Family Tree

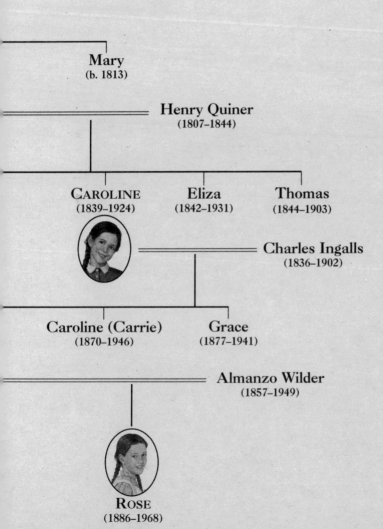

Mary
(b. 1813)

Henry Quiner
(1807–1844)

CAROLINE
(1839–1924)

Eliza
(1842–1931)

Thomas
(1844–1903)

Charles Ingalls
(1836–1902)

Caroline (Carrie)
(1870–1946)

Grace
(1877–1941)

Almanzo Wilder
(1857–1949)

ROSE
(1886–1968)

On Top
of
Concord Hill

STUTSMAN COUNTY LIBRARY
910 5TH ST S E
JAMESTOWN, N D 58401

WITHDRAWN

Maria D. Wilkes

Illustrations by Dan Andreasen

HarperTrophy®
An Imprint of HarperCollinsPublishers

Harper Trophy®, ☎®, Little House®, and The Caroline Years™
are trademarks of HarperCollins Publishers Inc.

On Top of Concord Hill
Text copyright © 2000 by HarperCollins Publishers Inc.
Illustrations © 2000 by Dan Andreasen
All rights reserved. No part of this book may be used or reproduced
in any manner whatsoever without written permission except in the case
of brief quotations embodied in critical articles and reviews.
Printed in the United States of America. For information address
HarperCollins Children's Books, a division of HarperCollins Publishers,
1350 Avenue of the Americas, New York, NY 10019.
www.littlehousebooks.com

Library of Congress Cataloging-in-Publication Data
Wilkes, Maria D.
  On top of Concord Hill / Maria D. Wilkes ; illustrations by Dan
Andreasen.
      p.   cm.
  Summary: After moving with their widowed mother to the home in
the woods near Concord, Wisconsin, nine-year-old Caroline Quiner, who
grows up to become the mother of Laura Ingalls Wilder, and her brothers
and sisters try to adjust to their new neighborhood and a new stepfather.
  ISBN 0-06-026999-5 — ISBN 0-06-027003-9 (lib. bdg.)
  ISBN 0-06-440689-X (pbk.)
  1. Ingalls, Caroline Lake Quiner—Juvenile fiction. [1. Ingalls,
Caroline Lake Quiner—Fiction.   2. Wilder, Laura Ingalls, 1867–1957—
Family—Fiction.   3. Frontier and pioneer life—Wisconsin—Fiction.
4. Stepfathers—Fiction.   5. Wisconsin—Fiction.]   I. Andreasen, Dan, Ill.
II. Title.
PZ7.W648389 On   2000   00-33585
[Fic]—dc 21   CIP
                                                                       AC

                    5   6   7   8   9   10
                               ❖
             First Harper Trophy edition, 2000

Author's Note

Before Laura Ingalls Wilder ever penned the Little House books, she wrote to her aunt Martha Quiner Carpenter, asking her to "tell the story of those days" when she and Laura's mother, Caroline, were growing up in Brookfield, Wisconsin. Aunt Martha sent Laura a series of letters that were filled with family reminiscences and vividly described the Quiners' life back in the 1800s. These letters have served as the basis for the books about Caroline Quiner, who married Charles Ingalls and became Laura's beloved Ma.

The Caroline Quiner Ingalls whom I've come to know through Aunt Martha's letters, personal accounts, and my own research is, I was surprised and delighted to discover, even more animated, engaging, and outspoken than the fictional Caroline whom millions of readers have grown to know and love. I have presented the most realistic account possible of Caroline Quiner's life while still remaining true to the familiar depiction of Ma in the Little House books.

—M.D.W.

Contents

On Top *of* Concord Hill

Signs

"We're going to town! We're going to town!" Eliza sang out as Caroline helped button up her red plaid dress. Eliza was two years younger, and the dress had been Caroline's the year before. Mother had tucked and hemmed it so that it now fit Eliza perfectly.

"Concord is not really a town." Caroline sighed. "Not like Brookfield."

Brookfield was thirty miles away. It was a proper town with a wagon maker's, a shoemaker's, a blacksmith's, and best of all a general store with shelves overflowing with everything anyone would ever want to buy. Brookfield was where Caroline had lived all her life until just last year. Now she lived deep in the woods, in a small house made of logs.

Concord was only two miles away. It was supposed to be a town, but it was really just a place where two roads crossed each other.

"Brookfield was not very big when Mother and Father first settled there," Martha said in her know-it-all voice. Ever since she had turned eleven, Martha had been acting very grown up. Now she whirled around, admiring how her pretty green sprigged calico skirt flounced about. Only Martha's dress was new. Martha had been allowed to pick the fabric from the bolts of cloth Zobey the peddler had brought in his leather sacks when he had come traipsing through the woods the month before. Martha was lucky. She was the oldest girl, and so she always got to wear the dresses first.

"Mother said there are lots of new settlers in these parts just like us," Martha continued matter-of-factly. "I bet we'll see all kinds of folks today at Camp Meeting."

Caroline felt a quiver of excitement run through her. They had not met many neighbors in the whole year they had lived in their little cabin surrounded by tall fir trees and thick oaks. But today was a special day. They were going to Concord for a Camp Meeting. Caroline did not really know what a Camp Meeting was. Mother said there would be preaching and singing, just like in church. Caroline knew there might also be marrying, although Mother had not said so.

Caroline bit her lip and glanced sideways at her sisters. She longed to tell them the secret she had been keeping for weeks. A secret no one, not even Mother, knew she was holding inside. Two months before, in April, Caroline had overheard something she knew she was not meant to hear. Standing just around the side of the cabin, Caroline had listened while Mr. Holbrook asked Mother to marry him.

Mr. Holbrook was one of Mr. Austin Kellogg's workers. Mother had been hired by

Mr. Kellogg, the richest man in Concord, to cook for these workers last year. Every day for several months, strange men had come into Caroline's home morning, noon, and night, and Mother had prepared food for them. Most of the men had been rough and very rude. They had terrible manners while they gulped down food at Mother's table. But Mr. Holbrook had been different. He was quiet and thoughtful. In his spare time he had helped the boys around the farm. At Christmas he had even bought them shiny panes of glass to put in the window frames, replacing the pieces of tanned deerskin they had stretched over the openings. Mr. Holbrook pretended that Santeclaus had brought the glass panes, but Caroline knew better.

Mother had not said yes or no to Mr. Holbrook's proposal. As Caroline had listened, Mother had told him that she would make her decision by the time the circuit rider came through Concord in June. The circuit rider was Reverend Speakes. And he would be preaching at Camp Meeting today.

"Are you girls ready?" Mother's voice rang out cheerfully from the bedroom she shared with the girls. Caroline turned to look, and as Mother stepped into the cabin's main room, she let out a little gasp.

All through the winter and spring Caroline had seen Mother in the same brown woollen dress and white apron every day. Now she wore her fine striped blue dress with the dainty lace trim around the collar. Tiny pearl buttons ran in a perfect line from her throat all the way down to her toes. The skirt flared out from Mother's perfectly slender waist in a lovely bell shape. Her long black hair had been brushed until it shone and was coiled back into a heavy twist.

"You're so pretty!" Eliza cried, rushing to touch the dress with careful fingers.

For weeks Caroline had been looking for signs that Mother was going to be married again. It had been five whole years since Father's ship had gone down in a terrible storm. Caroline missed Father very much. She thought about him every day. She did not know if she would like having a new father. Mr. Holbrook did not smile very much. He did not laugh and joke and sing the way Father had. But Caroline knew Mr. Holbrook was kind and gentle. He had done a great many nice things for them for no reason at all.

Now, as Caroline watched Mother give a playful little curtsey to Eliza, her green eyes sparkling, she wondered if this was a sign. Surely Mother wearing her very best dress and looking so happy meant that she had made her decision.

"Let me look at my pretty girls," Mother said, clapping her hands together.

Caroline stood in a row with her sisters, and Mother pulled at their sleeves and checked their hems one last time.

"I'm glad this dress still fits you," Mother said when it was Caroline's turn.

"Me too." Caroline smiled. The dress was a soft, shimmery blue. It had been Martha's last year, but for once Caroline hadn't minded getting Martha's hand-me-down. Caroline had loved the silky blue dress from the moment she had first seen it. Martha had worn it only a few times before she had grown too big for it. So it was almost new. The material felt cool against her clean skin. Caroline was glad they had had their baths the night before, even though it had only been Friday and not Saturday.

"Now quick, girls, time to braid your hair." Mother began to comb out Eliza's blond curls while Martha turned so Caroline could braid her straight brown hair.

"I wish Grandma could come with us today," Caroline said.

Mother nodded her head. "I wish your grandmother could be here too," she answered, and Caroline noticed that she looked thoughtful for a moment.

Grandma used to live with them in Brookfield. She was the one who had always combed and braided their hair in the morning. But now Grandma lived far away in Milwaukee with Uncle Elisha and his wife, Margaret, and their sons. She had never even seen the little cabin in the woods.

When all the braids were neat and the ribbons tied in perfect bows on the ends, Mother told the girls to wait quietly at the table in the big room and went back into the bedroom. Soon the boys came clomping down the ladder from the loft where they slept. They were dressed in their good white linen shirts and crisp dark-blue trousers and bright-red suspenders. Joseph's brown hair and little Thomas' golden locks were parted neatly and slicked down with bear grease. Only Henry's unruly sandy curls did not like to be tamed and stood out every which way on his head.

"I don't see why we have to get all gussied up and go to church on Saturday," Henry grumbled under his breath, pulling at his stiff collar.

Caroline gave Henry a stern look and glanced into the little bedroom, but Mother had not heard. She was gazing at herself in the small mirror propped up against the clothes chest, smoothing a few loose strands of hair.

Another sign!

"And I don't see why we have to wear our shoes," Henry continued, wrinkling his nose.

Caroline looked down at the tops of her scuffed black boots. They had been almost new two years ago, but now they were worn and tight in the toes. All summer long girls and boys went barefoot, and Caroline loved the feel of warm grass and earth between her toes. It felt strange to be wearing shoes in June. But she would not dare go to church without shoes. Martha had done that once in Brookfield and gotten into a whole heap of trouble.

Now Martha pretended she had never been bad. "It's only for one day, Henry," she said in her new grown-up voice.

"I heard this Camp Meeting goes on for *two* days," Henry replied. "So you'd better get used to pinched toes."

"What's this about pinched toes?" Mother asked in a worried voice as she came gliding through the doorway in her bell skirt.

"Nothing," Henry said quickly. No one really wanted to complain. There was no money for new shoes. And besides, there was no shoemaker in Concord.

Mother cocked her head but did not have time to press Henry further. There was a knocking at the door.

"That will be Mr. Holbrook," Mother said, and Caroline couldn't help but notice that Mother's cheeks flushed a soft pink and she fidgeted with the lace at her throat.

"Good morning, Charlotte," Mr. Holbrook said in his slow, deep voice, taking off his hat as he entered the cabin. He turned and gave a quick nod of his head. "Children."

Caroline had never seen Mr. Holbrook in anything but his work clothes. He had always looked tidy even when he was helping around the farm, but today he looked especially clean and neat in his dark coat and pantaloons. His square cheeks were closely shaven, and his long, dark hair was pulled back and tied with a thin piece of leather. The bushy strip of hair framing his jaw that always reminded Caroline of a furry caterpillar had been perfectly trimmed.

Caroline realized that Mr. Holbrook looked almost handsome, and she wondered if perhaps this was another sign. Why would he be so dressed up if he wasn't hoping to be married today?

"If you're ready, we'd best be on our way," Mr. Holbrook said, and his voice did not sound as certain as it usually did.

"Yes, I'm ready," Mother answered softly, slipping her pretty blue bonnet carefully over her hair and tying the strings in a bow beneath her chin. "Now, who will carry the basket and the blanket?"

Before Caroline could call out, Martha said, "I'll take the basket, Mother." Primly she tucked the basket of food onto her arm. Then Joseph stepped forward and took the clean horse blanket. Caroline was glad. She would have liked to carry the picnic basket, but it was too warm a day to carry an old wool blanket.

"Well then," Mother said. She glanced around the room and opened her mouth as if she were about to speak.

Caroline held her breath. Perhaps now the

secret would be out and she would no longer feel like she was bursting inside.

But after a second or two Mother closed her mouth again, and smiled. "I trust you will behave like little ladies and gentlemen" was all she said.

Caroline slowly let out her breath and reached for her bonnet. Perhaps Mother had still not decided whether she would marry Mr. Holbrook. Perhaps she would decide after all the preaching.

Outside the cabin, Wolf bounded up from his napping place under a shady tree and began to follow, but Caroline said in her stern voice, "Stay, Wolf. You can't come to church with us."

Wolf pricked up his ears and whined a little, but he was a good dog and did as he was told. Caroline slipped in behind Martha and Eliza as the family walked in a line down the little path that led through the leafy woods.

The afternoon air was already hot, but it was always cooler inside the forest. Overhead the great tall trees bobbed and swayed a little, their branches heavy with bluebirds and meadow-larks and speckle-breasted sparrows singing their sweet songs. Pairs of robins darted here and there along the lush green ground, and rabbits and other unseen creatures rustled through the ferns and thick brush.

As Caroline went along, she thought how good it felt to be all together walking through the summer woods. Every day for an entire year the whole family had worked very hard, clearing the land and planting and trying to make the little cabin more like home. And when Mother had taken on the job feeding Mr. Kellogg's men, there was always too much food to cook and too many dishes to wash to do anything but work. But today there was no work. It was just like Sunday, except that it was better because they were going on an adventure. Caroline was so happy, she suddenly felt like skipping and running, but she knew that ladies did not skip or run in their good dresses.

Eliza was only seven, and she did skip a little alongside Caroline.

"Will there be singing at Camp Meeting?" she asked breathlessly.

"I hope so," Caroline answered. She had loved all the singing in the little church in Brookfield. She wondered if they sang the same hymns in Concord. She wondered what the church looked like. They had been to Concord only once before, and she had not seen a church.

Eliza ran ahead to join Mother as Henry picked up a blade of grass and began blowing across it, making a whistling sound. He stopped to nudge Caroline. "You know where I'd like to be right now, Caroline?" he said in a quiet voice so Mother wouldn't hear. "I'd like to be knee-deep in the river, fishing for bluegill and shiners."

"Don't you want to meet our neighbors?" Caroline asked.

Henry shrugged and grinned his donkey grin. Caroline called it that because with his mouth open and all his teeth showing, he looked just like a friendly donkey. "Don't make no difference to me," he answered, and started whistling on the grass blade again.

"Don't you miss having neighbors like Charlie and Mr. Ben?" Caroline persisted, and Henry nodded but kept on whistling.

Mr. and Mrs. Ben Carpenter and their son, Charlie, had been their neighbors in Brookfield, and ever since Father had gone away, the Carpenters had always helped the family in whatever way they could. They had even come along when Uncle Elisha had brought the Quiners here to their new home. Charlie, Mr. Ben, as the children called him, and Uncle Elisha had stayed for three whole weeks, showing Henry and Joseph how to chop and girdle the trees and burn the brush in great piles. Mr. Ben and Uncle Elisha had laid down a wooden floor in the cabin and had built a small henhouse to keep the hens safe. But then the Carpenters had gone back to Brookfield and Uncle Elisha had gone back to Milwaukee. Now Caroline missed Mr. Ben's quick smile and his jolly laugh. She missed the way he told stories and sang silly songs.

Thinking about the Carpenters made Caroline

think about all the other Brookfield things she missed. She missed the two-story frame house they had lived in, and she missed the barn and the large henhouse. She missed the one tall tree by her bedroom window, and she missed the field of wildflowers stretching down to the river. She missed her friends from school, Anna and Elsa. Even with all her brothers and sisters around her, the woods sometimes seemed lonely. Most of all, she missed her father.

"I wonder what it will be like if—" Caroline stopped herself just in time. She had almost told her secret. She had almost wondered out loud what it would be like if Mr. Holbrook became their new father.

"You wonder what, Little Brownbraid?" Henry asked, tugging on her braid.

"Nothing," Caroline mumbled. The whole thing made her confused. She didn't even feel like scolding Henry for calling her by her old nickname. Father used to call Caroline Little Brownbraid when she was four years old. But now that Caroline was nine, she did not want to be called little anymore, even though she did still wear her hair in one long braid down her back.

"Do you like Mr. Holbrook?" Caroline asked instead, whispering it so that the others walking ahead would not hear.

Henry's face scrunched up into a scowl. "We sure never get a moment's rest when he's around," he said. "Even on a Sunday that fellow likes to keep busy."

Mother did not approve of working on the Sabbaday, but Mr. Holbrook had often come on Sunday to help around the farm. He worked for Mr. Kellogg during the week, and so Sunday was the only day he could lend a hand to Joseph and Henry.

"Come along, children. Now is not the time to dawdle," Mother's voice suddenly called back through the trees.

Caroline felt her cheeks grow hot. She did not think Mother and Mr. Holbrook could hear their words, but Mother always said it was not polite to whisper.

Henry went back to blowing on his grass whistle, and Caroline hurried ahead to walk with Martha and Eliza. She watched as Mother and Mr. Holbrook strolled along at the front of the line. They hardly spoke a word to each other as they walked, but every time they came to a bump or a log, Mr. Holbrook gently took Mother's elbow to steady her.

After a while they came out of the woods and turned onto the wide Territorial Road that led to Concord. The road was deeply rutted from the spring rains, and Caroline was surprised to see several wagons rolling slowly along, pitching to and fro as they tried to avoid the biggest bumps. Caroline had not seen anyone new in so long, it was hard not to stare at the men and women dressed in their Sunday clothes perched on the wagon seats. Sometimes there were little girls and boys sitting in the wagon beds. They stared back from their high places, looking pleased with themselves to be riding instead of walking along the dusty track like Caroline and her family.

"Folks are talking about making this a plank

road," Mr. Holbrook announced.

Henry's head perked up and he moved closer. "A plank road?"

"Mr. Kellogg says he wants to raise money to lay down planks from here to Watertown," Mr. Holbrook continued. "It would take a heap of men to lay down such a road."

"And a heap of planks," Joseph said.

"I reckon there's plenty of trees in these parts to lay down a track clear to Milwaukee," Mr. Holbrook said thoughtfully.

Caroline looked at the ground beneath her feet. Their house in Brookfield had been made of planks, but it was hard to imagine what a road made of planks would look like. She knew that if you stayed on this road, it would lead all the way to Milwaukee. She thought about walking on planks all the way to Uncle Elisha's house to visit Grandma.

"Mr. Kellogg has lots of plans for Concord," Mr. Holbrook continued. "He's set on building a mill so folks 'round here won't have to travel so far to grind their corn and wheat."

"What a good idea," Mother said.

Joseph and Henry seemed to be very interested in both the mill and the plank road. They began to ask Mr. Holbrook all kinds of questions, but Caroline stopped listening. They were drawing closer to Concord, and there were more people to look at. Some were in wagons and some were walking. Every once in a while Mother nodded her head to someone and said, "How do you do?"

There were more buildings along the road to look at as well. When she had come to Concord last year, Caroline had seen only one or two cabins, but now there were a few small frame houses and more cabins with split-rail fences edging the yards.

Soon they came to the crossroads that was the center of Concord. Mr. Holbrook turned right and led the way through a small patch of woods. Then suddenly they were in a great open field. The sky was a big, endless blue overhead, and Caroline felt like whirling around, but she made herself stand still and drink in all that openness. It had been a long time since she had seen so much blue. On their farm they had cleared land for planting, but it was just a little strip of earth compared to this huge field. Caroline had grown used to the trees like an enormous canopy always above her. Now she realized she had missed the sky.

"So many people!" Eliza said in a small voice, and it was true. The meadow was full of men and women and children. Some were standing, and others were sitting in large groups on the ground or on the tree stumps that still stuck up from the newly cleared earth. There were a great many wagons parked along the edge of the field, and Caroline even saw white canvas tents set up beside some of the wagons. She wondered what the tents were for.

Eliza tugged on Caroline's skirt as Mr. Holbrook led the way through the crowd. "Are we eating our picnic first?" she asked.

"I don't know," Caroline answered. It looked like everyone had brought picnic baskets or dinner pails, but no one was eating. The whole crowd seemed to be looking off toward one end of the field, where a platform made of planks sat slightly off the ground. There were poles sticking up, and a canvas had been stretched across the tops of the poles to make a little shelter from the sun.

"Where's the church?" Caroline asked.

Martha turned to her and laughed. "There's no church, silly. This is a Camp Meeting. They do the preaching out in the open."

Caroline felt her cheeks grow hot. She did not like to be laughed at, especially by Martha. No one had told her that Camp Meetings were out of doors.

"Greetings to you all on this glorious day," a warm, deep voice called out. "Won't you come join us?"

It was Mr. Kellogg, standing at the back of the crowd, beckoning to them. Caroline's heart began to race a little as the group made their way to him. She was always happy to see Mr. Kellogg. He was the most handsome man she had ever met, with his wavy black hair and smiling dark eyes and strong, clean-shaven jaw. He lived in a grand house on top of Concord Hill, and he always dressed in well-cut boughten clothes. Today was no exception. His gray jacket fit perfectly over a crisp white shirt and gray striped trousers. He wore a black felt hat on his head, and on his feet he did not wear boots like the other men, but black shoes made of what looked like the softest calfskin.

"Good to see you, friends," he said, taking Mr. Holbrook's hand in a firm shake and tipping his hat to Mother. Then he turned to Caroline and her sisters. "And how pretty your girls look today, Mrs. Quiner," he added.

"Thank you, sir," Caroline and Martha and Eliza answered all together.

Mr. Kellogg smiled and turned back to Mother. "Mrs. Quiner, I believe you've met my daughter, Margaret, but allow me to introduce my wife, Laura," he said.

Caroline had met Margaret several times. She was almost the same age as Eliza, but she looked younger because she was very small. Her tiny pointed face was framed by thick, bright-red hair. Today she wore a pretty, light-green dress with a pattern of tiny pink roses all over it.

Caroline had heard Margaret talk of her mother, but she had never seen her because she had been sick for many months. That was the reason Mother had cooked for Mr. Kellogg's workers—Mrs. Kellogg hadn't been well enough to do it herself. Now Caroline looked curiously at Mrs. Kellogg and decided she was exactly like a fine china doll. She was small like Margaret, and her skin was very pale. Red curls peeked out from her pretty yellow bonnet. Her dress was striped like Mother's, but the yellow-and-gold material was rich and silky. Her throat was covered in delicate lace, and even though it was such a warm day, she wore a shawl of knitted white cotton. She also wore white gloves, and she held a yellow silk parasol to shade herself from the sun. She did not sit on a blanket on the ground with Margaret, but on a little wooden chaise.

"How do you do?" she said in a soft, pretty voice. "Austin has told me so much about you all."

Mother and Mrs. Kellogg made small talk while the boys asked Mr. Kellogg about the mill and the plank road.

"The mill comes first," Mr. Kellogg said. "We'll need plenty of hands this summer to help dam up a part of the river so we can raise the mill."

"Me and my brother, we'd be happy to help, sir," Henry offered, and Mr. Kellogg put a hand on his shoulder.

"We'll certainly need all the help we can get, young man," he said.

As more and more people crowded onto the field, Mother told Joseph to spread out the blanket, and they settled down next to the Kelloggs to wait for the preaching to begin.

"Are all these folks our neighbors?" Eliza asked.

Mother shook her head. "I suspect some of them are," she answered. "But many people travel for miles around to hear the circuit rider. They camp overnight in the tents you saw at the edge of the clearing."

Caroline was glad to know what the tents

were for. She kept glancing around in every direction. It felt strange to be in the middle of so large a crowd and not know a soul except for Mr. Holbrook and the Kelloggs. In Brookfield she had known many people: the storekeeper and the blacksmith and the wagon maker and the schoolteacher, and of course the Carpenters and her friends at school. Thinking of school, she wondered if Mr. Kellogg would build a schoolhouse after he built his mill and his plank road. It seemed as if there were plenty of children around to fill a classroom. Caroline didn't mind studying with Mother at home, but she would prefer to go to a real school with real desks and a real teacher.

"It's awfully hot out here," Eliza whispered. "I wish I had a parasol like Mrs. Kellogg's."

Caroline nodded her head, imagining what it would be like to carry around a pretty parasol. Mother had trimmed a few to match the dresses she had made for some of the ladies in Brookfield, and she had even had one of her own when she had had a dress shop in Boston before she had married Father. But Mother did not have any now. All they had to keep them shaded from the midday sun beating down on their heads were their calico bonnets. Caroline was just wondering how long they would have to sit in the afternoon heat when suddenly there was a burst of sound that nearly made her jump out of her skin.

It was a harmonica, but the sound was brash and loud, rushing up to the treetops, then quivering and plunging down again. Caroline craned her neck to see over and around all the folks sitting and standing in front of her across the meadow. She caught sight of a figure dressed all in black making his way slowly along the edge of the crowd toward the little plank platform. He was followed by several men who were also dressed in black from head to toe. Caroline thought the men looked like big black crows all in a line on the bough of a tree.

Just as abruptly as it had started, the music stopped, and Caroline saw that the man playing the harmonica and the leader of the black crows was Reverend Speakes, who had dined with them in their cabin in April. Now he stood in the center of the platform and spread his arms up to the heavens.

"Rejoice!" he shouted at the top of his lungs. "Rejoice one and all!"

There was a hush and then another burst of harmonica. Concord's Camp Meeting had begun.

Camp Meeting

Reverend Speakes tapped his foot on the platform and let the harmonica dip down into a new song. The black crows stood in a row and led the crowd in a hymn. Caroline tried to follow along even though she did not know the words.

> *"I am bound for the promised land,*
> *I am bound for the promised land;*
> *Oh, who will come and go with me?*
> *I am bound for the promised land."*

After the music ended, there was another hush. Reverend Speakes slowly put his harmonica away in his breast pocket and then surveyed the crowd, a severe look on his face. Even from across the meadow Caroline could see how his eyes seemed to flash and burn.

The crowd waited silently. They leaned forward, all holding their breath at once. Then Reverend Speakes lifted one arm and pointed straight into the middle of the congregation.

"Are ye ready to be saved?" he shouted.

Several people in the crowd jumped up and threw their arms in the air and shouted loudly, "Yes!" and "We're ready!"

Caroline caught Martha's eye. Her sister looked just as bewildered as she felt. In their church in Brookfield there had been singing, but no one ever jumped up and shouted. You were supposed to sit quietly on your bench and listen to the preacher read from the Bible and talk about God.

But Reverend Speakes did not read and he did not talk. He shouted and shook and raged. Back and forth across the platform he strode, making the boards quiver beneath his weight. His face soon turned red, and sweat dripped from his forehead.

"If ye want to be saved, ye must first admit your sins." The preacher raised his arms into the air. "Only then shall ye be free!"

"Free!" many voices echoed.

"Admit your sins and watch them wash away," the preacher yelled.

"Wash away!" came the cry.

"Admit your sins and ye shall be saved!"

"Saved!" was the reply.

Caroline felt a chill go all the way down her spine. Nearly all the people around her except for Mother and Mr. Holbrook and the Kelloggs were standing and swaying and pounding their chests. Caroline had never seen grown-ups act this way. It frightened her, and she wished she could get up and run as fast as she could away from all the noise, or hide her face in Mother's lap, as Thomas was doing. But she knew she must sit still until Mother said it was time to go. She bunched the folds of her dress into her hands and tried to listen calmly as back and forth the shouting went, Reverend Speakes' voice and the crowd's responses beating out a monotonous rhythm.

After a time Caroline lost track of the words. The sun seemed to grow hotter and hotter. Then they were all singing once more, a song Caroline knew. She tried to join in, but her throat was dry and closed. As soon as the hymn was over, Reverend Speakes started yelling again, listing all the sins that needed to be washed away.

Reverend Speakes shouted about false pride and envy. Caroline glanced at Eliza and saw her biting her lip. Caroline did not think that wishing for Mrs. Kellogg's parasol meant that they were guilty of envy, but she wasn't sure.

Next, the reverend spoke of avarice.

"There is a terrible greed washing over our great land in this year of our Lord 1849," Reverend Speakes shouted. "I say to the men—and the women, too—thirsting for gold, moved by the devil to leave hearth and home and strike out for California and the promise of false riches, I say to ye, repent!"

Caroline noticed Henry shaking his head and crossing his arms over his chest, like he didn't agree with Reverend Speakes. She had heard him speaking earlier with Mr. Holbrook about how there was gold somewhere out west. She wondered if that made Henry a sinner.

"I say to those of you possessed by the twin evils of tobacco and liquor, repent and be saved!"

With a start Caroline remembered that Father used to smoke tobacco in his pipe after supper—and so did Mr. Holbrook! Did that mean they were both sinful and needed to be saved? She looked back at Mr. Holbrook, but he sat as solemnly as ever, staring straight ahead at the platform. She could not tell what he thought.

"Dancers!" Reverend Speakes shouted. "'Tis the devil's footsteps ye take. Repent ye of your sins and dance no more."

Caroline glanced at Mother now. Two years before, Mother had taught them all how to dance, and they had jigged the night away at Mrs. Stoddard's maple frolic in Brookfield.

Now Mother's face was pale, and Caroline wondered if she would begin to sway and fall to the ground like some of their neighbors. She hoped not.

"Gossips, listening for your neighbors' secrets and spreading lies. 'Tis the devil's work ye are doing. I tell ye now, repent and be saved."

Caroline felt a jolt like a thunderbolt run through her. *Listening for secrets.* She had not meant to hear Mr. Holbrook propose to Mother. It had been an accident. And she had told no one her secret, even though she had wanted to. Now that secret seemed to burn inside her like a red-hot coal. She closed her eyes, and when she opened them, it seemed that Reverend Speakes was looking straight at her, his blue eyes flashing fire.

Caroline began to tremble and gasp a little for air. Martha reached out and tugged on her arm. "What's the matter with you?" she whispered.

Caroline opened her mouth to speak, but her words were stuck inside. She was a sinner!

The reverend's voice cut through everything, speaking directly to her.

"I say, repent ye, sinners, while there is still time. I'm here to tell you that a great plague is coming. It shall wash the sinners away. It shall separate the wheat from the chaff. It is God Almighty sending his fiercest bolts of lightning. Repent now and be saved from His wrath."

One after another, clusters of townsfolk fell to their knees and threw their hands in the air. Some began to roll on the ground, shaking and sobbing. Many of the babies in the crowd had begun to cry, and their piercing wails mixed with the other cries. Caroline closed her eyes again. She did not think she could sit still any longer. Her whole body was shaking now, as she thought about how she was chaff and would be washed away. Then she felt a firm hand on her shoulder, and she looked up into Mother's eyes.

"Let's go, Caroline," Mother said, holding a crying Thomas by the hand.

Caroline saw that they were all standing,

waiting for her. On wobbly legs she got up and followed as Mother pressed through the throng of people. The Kelloggs were already gone, and several other families were leaving the field as well.

Reverend Speakes' voice seemed to follow them as Mr. Holbrook led the way onto the road. Caroline flinched at each shout, as if the voice were burning into her. When they came to the crossroads, the voice finally stopped, and the harmonica started up again. Voices were raised in song.

"Free at last, free at last,
I thank God I'm free at last.
Free at last, free at last,
I thank God I'm free at last."

As the song faded away behind them, Caroline heard Mother speaking soothingly to Thomas.

"It's all right," Mother said, and when Martha spoke up and asked if they were staying to meet their neighbors, Mother shook her head.

"I think we've heard enough preaching for one day. We'll have to meet our neighbors another time."

Caroline was surprised. In Brookfield Mother had never left church early. But there had never been so much shouting and wailing as there had been today. Caroline wondered if Mother was as frightened as she was by the preacher's words. She looked up to see Henry's donkey grin.

"Whew!" he said. "I never seen so much carrying on in all my born days. If that's the way our neighbors worship, I'm glad we didn't stick around to meet them."

"Mother says the folks are from all over, not just our neighbors," Martha said. She was holding on to Eliza's hand, and Eliza's blue eyes were as big as saucers.

"Was the man in black the devil?" Eliza asked in a scared voice.

Martha shook her head. But Caroline thought what Eliza had said was true. Reverend Speakes had seemed like the devil himself, dressed all in black and shouting at the top of his lungs.

She began to shiver again, even though the sweat was running down her back.

By the time they came to the place to turn off the Territorial Road, Thomas had forgotten about his tears. He ran down the path in front of Mother and Mr. Holbrook, zigzagging between the tree trunks.

Caroline was glad to be back in woods, with the trees to shelter her from the sun, and to shelter her from the preacher's words. She could hear singing far in the distance, but it was soft now and sounded almost like angels.

"The man in black said dancing was a sin," Eliza whispered. "Is it a sin?"

"Of course not," Martha answered. "Mother taught us how to dance herself. Mother would never do anything that was a sin."

Caroline wanted to ask Martha what she thought about listening for secrets, and if Martha thought that overhearing Mother's conversation with Mr. Holbrook made her a sinner. But wouldn't that make her even more of a sinner, gossiping about things she wasn't meant to know? Caroline felt her insides twisting into a knot as they came to the clearing. Wolf bounded toward her, wagging his bushy tail and barking loudly.

"Good boy," Caroline said, rubbing his fur and letting him lick her hands. She had really wanted to go to Concord and meet her neighbors. But now she was glad to be home. She leaned down and gave Wolf a hug.

Inside the cabin, Mother took off her bonnet and smoothed back her hair. "Well, it seems a shame to waste such a glorious day and a picnic supper." Her voice sounded happy. "Hurry and change out of your church clothes, children. We'll eat our picnic down by the river."

"Yahoo!" Henry shouted, but Mother quickly shushed him.

Mr. Holbrook looked around uncertainly. He held his hat in his hands. "I think I'd best be heading home," he said. "There's a heap of work to do around my place."

"Won't you join us, Frederick?" Mother asked, and Caroline looked up in surprise. She was not used to hearing Mother call Mr.

Holbrook by his first name. Earlier today Caroline would have counted this as another sign pointing to a wedding. Now she wondered if all the shouting at Camp Meeting had made Mother decide not to marry Mr. Holbrook.

"Well, I reckon me and the boys could do a little fishing while we're at the river," Mr. Holbrook said after a moment. Mother's green eyes smiled at him, and he seemed to almost smile back.

Henry seemed near bursting, wanting to shout out. But he only grinned and then rushed toward the ladder. All at once Caroline felt like giggling. Henry had gotten his wish after all. Soon he would indeed be knee-deep in the river, fishing pole in hand.

As quickly as they could, Mother and the girls changed back into their everyday dresses. Caroline felt only a little sad. She loved dressing up in her pretty clothes. But it felt good to wriggle into her worn calico. She felt like she could breathe again.

When they went outside, the boys already

had their fishing poles. Once more they all set out through the woods, but this time Caroline ran along with Eliza. Even Martha picked up her skirts and rushed amid the trees, laughing and calling out to the boys. They were no longer proper ladies in their church dresses. The scariness of Camp Meeting melted away.

At the river Mr. Holbrook took off his jacket and hung it carefully from a tree branch. He rolled up his trouser legs, and for the rest of the sunny afternoon he and the boys fished along the grassy banks. Caroline, Martha, and Eliza held up their skirts and waded into the water, letting the coolness lap against their ankles. Caroline longed to jump in and let the water wash over her. But she did not want to be wearing only her petticoats in front of Mr. Holbrook.

After a while Mother said it was time to eat. Thomas came rushing back down the river. He had caught two small fish, and Joseph and Mr. Holbrook had caught a few, but Henry had caught the most. He held up his line of bluegill and shiners for everyone to see.

"Your boys are mighty good fishermen," Mr. Holbrook said. "A man will never go hungry as long as he knows how to fish."

The boys went to gather kindling while Mr. Holbrook whittled a few long sticks with his knife. In no time there was a roaring little fire and they were roasting up the boys' catch.

Caroline and Martha helped Mother set out the picnic supper on the wool blanket under a big oak. The light fluttered across Caroline's hands as she set out the hard-boiled eggs and cold beans and corn bread.

Now they would have fish, too. Caroline's mouth began to water as the smell of fish smoking over the fire wafted into the air.

When everything was ready, they sat, eating quietly and watching the light change over the river. Everything tasted wonderful. For a special treat Mother had even made little round cakes out of white sugar. There was one cake for each of them, and Caroline nibbled slowly on hers to make it last.

Mr. Holbrook commented on the good food and thanked Mother for preparing it. Mother smiled and nodded at the compliment. Caroline thought it was a nice feeling to have Mr. Holbrook there among them on such a pleasant outing.

As the shadows began to grow and lengthen across the water, Mother said it was time to go. They packed up the dishes and folded up the blanket and headed back through the woods. Nighthawks dipped and spiraled through the trees, and gray squirrels scurried along the branches. The cicadas were droning their loud, dull hum.

Back at the cabin the boys went to fill the wood box, and Martha and Eliza headed inside. Caroline paused outside the door. Mother and Mr. Holbrook had stopped at the edge of the garden, and they were talking quietly and seriously. She stood for a moment wondering what Mother and Mr. Holbrook could be saying when, with a jolt, Reverend Speakes' voice was inside her head again.

Listening for secrets. 'Tis the devil's work.

Caroline rushed into the cabin. She must be a terrible sinner to want to listen again to other people's words. Her heart was beating fast, and her whole body felt hot and shivery, the way it had at Camp Meeting. She went about her evening chores, helping to wash the tin plates and cups, putting them away in the dish dresser, seeing to the hens in the henhouse and the geese in their pen. But all the while, she was thinking about how she had been a sinner and hadn't even repented when she had had the chance.

Secrets

The moon shone softly through the glass windowpanes, giving the little bedroom a peaceful glow. But Caroline felt anything but peaceful. She tossed and turned on the straw tick beside Martha and Eliza. She closed her eyes tightly and opened them again. Her sisters' breathing had been slow and steady for some time now. Even Joseph and Henry had finished their game of checkers long ago and joined little Thomas in the loft. Caroline could hear Henry's deep snores from up above. The sound mingled with

Mother's soft voice, singing as she rocked to and fro in the big room.

"We shall sing on that beautiful shore
The melodious song of the blest,
And our spirits shall sorrow no more,
Not a sigh for the blessing of rest."

It was one of Caroline's favorite songs. She loved the way Mother's voice rolled smoothly up and down over the notes. Caroline tried to let the melody carry her to sleep, but each time she closed her eyes, she saw Reverend Speakes' face, his eyes glowing in the dark like red-hot coals. In her head, the song Mother was singing seemed to mix with the last song Caroline had heard as the family left Camp Meeting.

Free at last, free at last,
I thank God I'm free at last.

Caroline's eyes flew open. All of a sudden she knew she wanted to be free of this feeling of being a sinner. Quietly, so Eliza and Martha would not hear her, Caroline slipped out of bed and tiptoed in bare feet across the plank floor. The door was already open a crack, and she peered out into the big room.

Mother was seated in her rocking chair by the hearth. She moved slowly back and forth, her sewing needle glinting in the firelight.

Everything in the room glowed, neat and tidy. The heavy iron cookstove sat beside the hearth, the pots and pans stacked on top. The dish dresser was on the opposite side of the small window, all the dishes and cups put away for the night. The oak chairs were pushed under the solid oak table, and the china washbasin sat on its wooden stand near the heavy log door, which was closed tightly against the night.

Caroline pulled a little at the bedroom door, and it creaked hoarsely. The rocker stopped at once, and Mother's head shot up, a look of concern already on her face.

"What is it, Caroline?" she asked. "Are you not feeling well?"

Caroline closed the door behind her and padded across the room until she was standing before Mother. Everything was once more tied up in knots inside her. She thought of all the people falling to the ground at Camp Meeting, and tears came to her eyes.

Mother put her sewing aside and took Caroline's hands in her own.

"Is this about Reverend Speakes?" Mother asked gently. "He frightened you this afternoon, didn't he?"

Slowly Caroline nodded her head.

"He frightened me too," Mother said, and Caroline looked up in surprise. A shadow of a smile passed over Mother's face. "Only once before have I heard a preacher speak in such a way. I was a child in Boston. Like Reverend Speakes, this preacher screamed and fussed so much, he near frightened me out of my wits."

Caroline took a deep breath. "Reverend Speakes said dancing was a sin." This wasn't really what she wanted to talk about, but she wasn't quite ready to tell Mother about her listening for secrets.

Mother looked thoughtful for a moment before speaking. "There are some people who believe that dancing is a sin. But that is not the way I was raised. To my understanding, dancing is one of the happiest gifts God gives us. It seems to me that doing away with dancing would be like"—Mother's green eyes searched the room—"like banishing the sun."

Caroline remembered how Father sometimes used to pick her up and whirl her around the room in the little frame house in Brookfield, his deep voice raised to the rafters, singing a happy tune.

"Did Father like to dance?" Caroline asked.

Mother's face was smiling and sad all at once.

"Yes, Caroline, your father was a fine dancer."

"Do you think Mr. Holbrook likes to dance?" Caroline asked before she could stop herself. Mother's eyes fixed on her, and all of a sudden Caroline felt a whooshing inside, as if all the knots in her stomach were unraveling at once, and the words came tumbling out: the secret she had kept for two long months, and the fear that she was doomed, as Reverend Speakes had said, for listening to secrets.

"Goodness," Mother said when Caroline had finally run out of things to say. "What a lot of worries for such a little girl." She reached into her skirt pocket, pulled out her clean red kerchief, and handed it to Caroline so she could wipe her cheeks and blow her nose. Mother stood up and pushed the coals closer to the log with the iron tongs. She watched the fire for a while before turning back to Caroline and leading her to the table so they both could sit.

"It is true what Reverend Speakes said, Caroline." Mother spoke in a gentle voice. "Eavesdropping and gossiping are wrong. But I know you did not mean to hear what Mr. Holbrook and I were discussing, did you?"

"No, ma'am!" Caroline cried. She had just happened to hear Mr. Holbrook's proposal. She had not even understood what Mr. Holbrook had been saying at first.

"And you did not gossip about our conversation with your sisters and brothers, isn't that true?" Mother asked.

"No, ma'am, I did not," Caroline answered, shaking her head fiercely. She had wanted to, but she had not.

Mother put her hand over Caroline's on the table. "You are not sinful, Caroline. I know you to be a good girl. I am proud of you. Your father would have been proud of you too."

The knots were all gone, and Caroline felt something warm and glowing melting through her.

"Now, I will tell you something I was going to tell you all in the morning." Mother paused. "It is true that Mr. Holbrook has asked me to marry him. And I have consented."

Caroline's eyes went wide. She waited for Mother to continue.

"He is a good man," Mother said slowly. "I think he will be a good father to you all." She squeezed Caroline's hand tightly. "He cannot replace your own father. You will always hold memories of him here." She reached out and touched Caroline's heart. "As will I."

They were silent for a while, listening to raindrops splatter against the window panes. Caroline did not remember when it had started to rain.

"Now off to bed with you," Mother said in a gentle but firm voice. "Sleeping time is wasting."

Slowly Caroline stood up. "Mother?"

"Yes, child?"

"May I ask one more question?"

"Yes, Caroline."

"Henry said Camp Meeting goes on for two days. Will Reverend Speakes marry you tomorrow? Will we be going back to Concord?"

Mother shook her head. "We will not be going back to Camp Meeting tomorrow. Neither Mr. Holbrook nor I cared for Reverend Speakes' style of preaching, and we do not want him to marry us. Mr. Kellogg is a justice of the peace. Perhaps he will agree to marry us. But not tomorrow." Mother stood and picked up her sewing again. "Now, no more questions."

Quietly Caroline slipped back into the bedroom and under the covers beside Eliza. She listened to see if her sisters had awakened, but their breathing was still deep and measured.

The room was black now. The clouds had swallowed up the moon. Caroline listened to the rain beating harder against the glass panes. She thought about how carefully Mr. Holbrook had put them into their frames last spring, how he had continued to pretend they were from Santeclaus when everyone knew he was the one who had brought them.

Closing her eyes, Caroline realized she still had the secret tucked inside, the thing no one else in the cabin knew besides Mother. But the secret did not feel heavy now. She was drifting off into a deep, dark place when suddenly someone was shaking her awake again.

"Caroline Lake Quiner, are you going to sleep all day?" Martha's voice rang out.

Caroline sat up and rubbed her eyes. She

could hardly believe it was morning already. Martha and Eliza were pulling their dresses on over their petticoats. Caroline felt like laughing as she watched Martha hurry to put on her apron. Only last year Martha had hated to get up early. She would lie in bed until the last possible minute. Now she was the one rushing to help Mother with breakfast.

Outside it was gray and wet, the rain coming down in gentle but steady drops. The boys had already brought in the water for the washbasin. Caroline waited until it was her turn to wash her face and hands. In summer the water was not heated over the fire the way it was in the winter. The cool wetness felt good on Caroline's sleepy face.

Mother was busy at the cookstove, frying up the fat pork and the cornmeal mush. She gave a little smile when Caroline came near to take the plates and mugs from the dish dresser.

"Did you sleep well, Caroline?" Mother asked.

"Yes, ma'am," Caroline answered. Now it felt special to share a secret with Mother. As she set the plates and mugs around the table, Caroline glanced at her sisters. She wondered what they would say when Mother told them the news.

When the food was on the table, Joseph, Henry and Thomas came in from the rain. They stood just outside the door, shaking the wet from their hats and wiping their muddy boots.

"The garden is getting a good drink," Joseph announced.

"As long as it's a drink and not a great big gulp, like last year," Henry said.

"This is just a day's rain, I think," Joseph said. He nodded confidently at Mother. Caroline shuddered to think about the terrible storm that had wiped away their crops last year. There had been so little left to harvest, they might have starved to death had it not been for Mr. Kellogg and the work he gave Mother.

"Let us eat now, children," Mother urged. They bowed their heads as Mother said the blessing. As usual, Henry was the first to reach for his fork.

STUTSMAN COUNTY LIBRARY
910 5TH ST S E
JAMESTOWN, N D 58401

"Use the sugar syrup sparingly, children. That's the last of it, I'm afraid," Mother said.

When it was her turn, Caroline carefully drizzled just a little of the thick, sweet maple syrup over her fried mush. Sugar syrup was one of Caroline's favorite things in the whole world. It made the everyday mush taste like a treat. They had had plenty while Mother was cooking for Mr. Kellogg's workers. But now the crock was low. Perhaps there would be more next spring when Mr. Kellogg tapped his maple trees again.

As they ate, Joseph talked to Mother about the crops and their plans for clearing the rest of the land for next year.

"We'll need to clear a heap more acres if we're to have a good wheat crop," Joseph said.

"Well, I sure hope Mr. Ben is planning on coming back, because I can't see doing it all ourselves," Henry said. Then he turned and winked at Caroline. "Even if Caroline comes out to help us."

Last year Caroline had helped drag the small trees and brush to the piles the men had turned into bonfires. Martha had stayed inside the kitchen with Mother, so Caroline had felt as if she had to work extra hard. For days after, her hands had been red and sore and her back had ached. She had torn and dirtied her dress so badly that she'd had to spend a whole day with Mother scrubbing and mending it. Mother had reluctantly agreed to let Caroline work in the fields because of all there was to do, but she did not like to see her girls toiling in such a way.

"I don't think you'll need Caroline this year," Mother said. "Mr. Holbrook will be here to help."

"We won't get much done if he only comes on Sundays," Henry scoffed.

Mother put her fork and knife down beside her plate. "I have something to tell you all," she said.

Everyone stopped eating, even Henry. They waited in silence for Mother to speak. Caroline knew the secret was finally about to be let out into the open.

"Mr. Holbrook has asked me to marry him,"

Mother said simply. "And I have agreed."

No one said a word. For several minutes the only sound was the rain outside and the ticking of the mahogany clock on the mantel. Caroline gave a quick glance around the table. Her brothers and sisters were all staring at Mother. Henry's mouth had fallen open. Only little Thomas seemed unconcerned.

"Mr. Holbrook whittled sticks by the river," he piped up. "Do you think he can whittle me a wooden man to go with my wooden horsie?"

Mother's face warmed and a smile passed over her lips. "If you ask him politely, I'm sure he will," she replied. She looked from one to the other of them, pausing on Henry last as she spoke. "I hope you will all be joyful and welcome Mr. Holbrook into our home."

Joseph cleared his throat. "When will you be married, Mother?"

"We were planning to have Reverend Speakes marry us after Camp Meeting today," Mother answered.

"We're going back there?" Henry cried out in disbelief. "To all that ranting and carrying on?"

"No, Henry, after yesterday we have decided not to go back to Camp Meeting," Mother said firmly. "We will speak to Mr. Kellogg. He is a justice of the peace. Perhaps he will marry us."

"So there'll be a real wedding?" Martha blurted out. "Will Grandma and Uncle Elisha come? And Cha— I mean the Carpenters? Will there be a party?"

Mother shook her head. "I have written to your grandmother and uncle telling them of my decision. But there will be no visiting and no party. I'm afraid we're all much too busy."

Martha slumped a little in her seat, disappointed. Joseph and Henry asked no more questions. Slowly they all went back to finishing up breakfast. Caroline barely tasted the food on her plate. Even though she had known the secret for so long, it felt different to have it out in the open. Somehow, Mother's telling everyone had made Caroline realize she was going to have a new father, and she did not know what she thought about that.

For the rest of the day there was a strange, quiet feeling inside the cabin. After breakfast Caroline and Martha and Eliza made the beds and swept the floors, barely saying a word. Later Caroline went outside into the drizzle to feed the geese and hens and to check for eggs. Even on a Sunday and even in the rain, the hens and geese must be seen to. But the rest of the day was spent indoors. Mother read to them from the Bible. Caroline and Martha worked on their nine-patch quilts while Eliza worked on her sampler. The boys whittled kindling by the fire. Everyone spoke politely to one another, and there was no whispering about Mother's news.

The mahogany clock slowly ticked out the long minutes of that day. Every once in a while Caroline stood up to stretch her legs. She went to the open doorway and peered into the gloom. She wondered if Reverend Speakes was preaching that very moment, rain and all. She held her breath and tried to hear the singing through the woods. But she knew Concord was too far away and the rain was like a blanket over everything.

At last it was time for bed. The rain had finally stopped, and it had left the night air cool and damp. Eliza snuggled close to Caroline under their quilt.

"Will Mr. Holbrook sleep in the loft with the boys?" Eliza whispered.

"Of course not," Martha said from her side of the bed.

"Where will he sleep?" Eliza persisted.

Martha was quiet for a while, and then she said, "I don't know. The cabin will be a sight more crowded though, I expect."

"Maybe Mr. Holbrook will build us a frame house like Father did in Brookfield," Eliza said. "Do you think so, Caroline?"

"Maybe he will," Caroline replied, and closed her eyes. She could hear Mother's soft voice, singing about the sweet by and by. There were no secrets now. Only questions. When would Mr. Holbrook become their new father, and how would things change inside the little cabin?

"Wednesday Best Day
of All"

T he next morning everyone went about
the chores as usual. After a day of so
much quiet it felt good to be busy
again. Caroline knew that her brothers and sisters were just as uncertain as she was about
the changes to come. Still, the air inside the
little cabin seemed to crackle and pop with the
promise of something new about to happen.

After seeing to the geese and hens, Caroline
went back inside to help Martha pour the

buckets of water Joseph and Henry had carried from the river into the big iron kettle over the fire. Monday was washday. Usually Caroline did not like scrubbing and rinsing, because it was such hard work, but today she did not mind. She hummed along with Mother as she helped separate the dark clothing from the light.

"Is Mr. Holbrook coming today?" Eliza timidly asked what Caroline herself had been wondering.

"I'm sure he'll stop by," Mother answered calmly as she stirred the white clothes into the pot of boiling water.

"Will you be married then?" Eliza asked.

"No, Eliza," Mother answered. "Mr. Holbrook is sure to bring news of Mr. Kellogg. We'll have to wait and see when he's free to marry us."

Mother stopped stirring to wipe the strands of dark hair away from her wet brow, and Caroline noticed that her face looked content. Caroline thought about the many months, especially right after Father's death, when Mother had been sad and tired all the time.

Perhaps Mr. Holbrook was not as jolly as Father had been, but Caroline knew he would make things easier for Mother.

By the time all the clothes had been scrubbed and rinsed clean, it was nearly time for dinner. While Mother twisted and wrung the last drops of water from the clothing, Martha, Caroline and Eliza put out the dinner things. There would be cold beans and leftover fried mush from the morning.

The boys came in from clearing trees, streaked with mud. After they washed up and everyone sat down at the table, Mr. Holbrook suddenly appeared at the open doorway. Mother jumped up to greet him, but Caroline and her brothers and sisters sat in silence. No one knew what to say. Mr. Holbrook himself seemed to hesitate before wiping his boots and coming inside. He took off his hat and held out a large brown jug for Mother.

"Fresh milk from Addie," Mr. Holbrook said.

Addie was Mr. Kellogg's cow. Caroline's

heart skipped a beat. Mr. Holbrook must have seen Mr. Kellogg. He must be bringing news about the wedding.

"Goodness gracious," Mother exclaimed, taking the jug and setting it on the table. "That's far too generous of Mr. Kellogg. I'll have you bring over some fresh eggs on your way back."

"It was Mrs. Kellogg insisted I bring it," Mr. Holbrook said, and Mother cocked her head to one side. "Mr. Kellogg was called away suddenly last night on family business."

"How long will he be gone?" Mother asked.

"Mrs. Kellogg said there's no way to tell for sure," Mr. Holbrook answered. "It could be a fortnight or more."

Caroline and Martha exchanged quick glances. So Mother would not be married for a whole fourteen days at least!

"Well," Mother said, then rested a hand on Mr. Holbrook's arm. "Please join us for dinner, Frederick. I've told the children."

Mr. Holbrook glanced around, and Caroline noticed the skin above his caterpillar beard flushing pink. Caroline gave him her warmest smile. He seemed to almost smile back, then gave a quick nod of his head. "Well, then," he said, and that was all.

Mother poured out the fresh milk into tin cups for everyone and set the rest aside to make butter. They had not had butter for several weeks. While Mother was feeding Mr. Kellogg's workers, Addie had been their cow. Mr. Holbrook had helped them build a pole barn to keep her out of the cold weather. When spring came and Mother's job was over, Mr. Kellogg had taken Addie back. Every once in a while Mother traded eggs for some of Addie's milk. But Caroline longed for the time when they would have a cow of their own so they would have fresh milk and butter every day.

Mother said the blessing, and they all began to eat. Quietly Caroline nibbled at the cold dinner and sipped the delicious milk. Martha and Eliza were silent, trying not to stare at Mr. Holbrook. Henry looked almost angry. Only Joseph and Thomas seemed to be at ease. Joseph and Mr. Holbrook spoke about

the mill again. Mr. Holbrook said that as soon
as Mr. Kellogg returned, all the men for miles
around would begin work on damming a part
of the river.

"Can we help, Mother?" Henry asked. "We
told Mr. Kellogg we would."

Mother glanced at Mr. Holbrook.

"*May* we help," she corrected, and then she
said, "We'll see."

"Seems to me there's plenty of work for
you boys to do around here," Mr. Holbrook
said.

Henry looked from Mother to Mr. Holbrook
and back again to Mother, but Mother did not
say anything more. Henry frowned into his
bowl of beans.

"Will you whittle me a wooden man for my
horsie?" Thomas asked suddenly, and Caroline
almost choked on her mush.

Mr. Holbrook carefully wiped at his whiskers
with the napkin before he spoke. "I might
could do that one of these evenings," he said,
and his face seemed to soften a bit.

After everything was eaten, Mr. Holbrook

cleared his throat and thanked Mother for a fine dinner. He headed out across the clearing, with Joseph, Henry, and Thomas following behind.

Mother went back to the washing, and Caroline helped Martha and Eliza hang the clothes out to dry. The morning sun had been very warm, and there were dry patches of leaves and grass, although the ground in the clearing still shimmered with puddles.

"So now there's time to plan for a real wedding," Martha said as soon as they were out of earshot of Mother. Her voice jumped with excitement.

"Mother said there wouldn't be a party," Caroline reminded her.

"But surely, if Mr. Kellogg does the marrying, Mother will at least make a special meal," Martha reasoned. "Maybe Mrs. Kellogg and Margaret will come too. So it will almost be like a party."

Caroline's face lit up. What Martha said had to be true. The Kelloggs had been very good to them. Surely Mother would want to do something special if they came to the wedding.

"Now, when I get married," Martha continued, "I will have a grand party with lots of folks from miles around. And there will be lots of eating and dancing."

"And what will Charlie say to that?" Caroline teased as she laid another shirt out to dry.

Martha's face turned a bright pink, but she kept smiling. Everyone knew that Martha especially liked Charlie Carpenter. While they had been neighbors, Martha had always made some excuse to run off with the boys so she could be near Charlie. Charlie was just like his father. He had a quick smile and a friendly laugh. He was always joking or singing songs while he worked.

"When *I* get married, I'll ride in a fine carriage." Eliza began to prance around a large oak tree, as if she were indeed being carried in grand style.

Caroline thought for a moment. She had been to only one party, the maple frolic in Mrs. Stoddard's house in Brookfield. And the only wedding she had ever heard about was when Mother had married Father long ago. Mother had not mentioned a party when she told the story of how Father had been very late to the preacher's house. When he had finally arrived, Mother saw that there had been a terrible accident. Father had badly burned his hand in his silversmith shop, making beautiful silver candlesticks for Mother as a wedding gift. That was why he had been so late.

"I wonder if Mr. Holbrook will bring Mother a present," Caroline said thoughtfully.

"Nothing so fine as the candlesticks," Martha replied. "Now, let's hurry and finish these clothes. Mother will surely be calling us soon."

That night Mr. Holbrook did not come for supper, but he arrived early the next day while Caroline was gathering eggs. Caroline watched him stride purposefully across the yard and into the cabin. After only a few moments he came out again and walked back through the woods. Caroline continued to search for eggs and was just reaching for her fourth when

Martha came rushing up to the henhouse.

"The wedding will be tomorrow!" she cried.

"Tomorrow?" Caroline squeaked. "Is Mr. Kellogg back already?"

Martha shook her head. "No, but Mr. Holbrook says there's another justice of the peace who can do the marrying. His name is Delos Hale, and he wants to do it tomorrow because after that he's busy getting ready to head off to California for the gold rush."

Caroline could only stare at Martha, trying to make sense of what she was saying.

"Mother says to hurry and bring in all the eggs you find," Martha continued. "There's plenty to do before folks come tomorrow."

"But . . . but . . . who's coming?" Caroline stammered.

Martha let out an exasperated sigh. "I told you. Mr. Hale is coming, and there has to be a witness, so he'll be bringing his wife along too." Martha's eyes sparkled, and she gave a big smile. "So it will be a party after all!" Then she turned around and hurried off.

Quickly Caroline checked the rest of the boxes. When she left the henhouse, she had seven eggs. She wondered if Mother would make something special with them for the Hales.

Inside the cabin, Mother was a whirl of motion in her brown skirt and white apron. Her face was flushed, and her eyes darted around the room finding things to do. Tuesday was usually ironing day, but today there would be ironing and churning and baking and scrubbing all at once.

Mother flew about, telling the girls what to do. First, Caroline and Martha took turns at the butter churn while Eliza helped Mother at the mixing bowl.

"Thank goodness for fresh milk and hens a-laying," Mother said as she began to mix together the last of the white flour and the molasses and eggs.

As Caroline pumped the butter churn up and down, she chanted the little song Grandma had taught her:

"Come, butter, come,
  Come, butter, come.
  Peter standing at the gate
  Waiting for a butter cake.
  Come, butter, come."

At last the creamy yellow butter began to separate. Martha helped pour off the buttermilk, and Caroline rinsed the butter well and salted it. She pressed some of the golden lumps into the butter molds, and the rest went into Mother's mixing bowl.

Mother told Eliza go into the root cellar and get the very last jar of blueberry preserves, so Caroline knew Mother was making her special blueberry cake. Her mouth began to water just thinking about taking a bite of sweet cake mixed with tangy blueberries. It had been so long since she had tasted it.

With the delicious smell of the cake in the oven filling the cabin, Mother and the girls set about cleaning the rooms from top to bottom. They had tidied that morning, but now they scrubbed the floors and aired out the straw ticks and polished the pewter dishes and wiped the glass windows until everything was spotless and shining. Then Mother had the girls pull out their church dresses again to check for any stains or tears from Saturday. After supper Henry and Joseph again hauled water from the river for bathing.

"Two baths in one week!" Henry complained loudly.

But Caroline was glad when it was her turn to sit in the tin tub behind the screen made by stringing a blanket across two chairs. And after so much excitement, she was happy to curl up on the newly fluffed straw tick beside her sisters at nightfall. She fell asleep right away and woke as soon as the first light began to peep through the window.

Mr. Holbrook had said he would bring the Hales just before dinnertime, so they all rushed to do their chores. Joseph had caught a plump jackrabbit, and the girls helped Mother dress it with her special onion-and-bread stuffing.

There were already summer peas from the garden, and there were green tomatoes. Mother took a few from the vine and fried them with cornmeal.

The girls went outside to gather wildflowers. They held up their bouquets of bluebells and hollyhocks and black-eyed Susans, and Mother took them with a warm smile.

"How lovely," she said, putting them together into a pitcher.

Then Caroline helped spread Mother's fine linen cloth over the table and set out the heavy pewter plates and cups. Last to go on the table were Father's silver candlesticks. Caroline took one while Martha held the other. Seeing the candlesticks suddenly made a lump form in Caroline's throat. But she remembered Mother's words. Father would always be there in her heart.

When it was nearly noon, everyone hurried into their good clothes once more. Mother changed back into her pretty striped blue dress, and Caroline watched as she fixed her hair in front of the mirror. Mother had that faraway look in her eyes again. Her face was pale, and she fumbled a little with the hair-pins.

Soon voices could be heard through the trees. Caroline and Martha and Eliza rushed to the window. They could see Mr. Holbrook walking slowly down the path, an older couple by his side. The man wore a dark-brown suit with a red-striped vest over his large belly, and he walked with a silver-tipped cane. The lady was dressed in a shimmery gray silk dress with lace around the collar. She held a gray parasol overhead. They were both short and round and had silvery-white hair.

"Come away from the window, girls," Mother scolded.

Caroline went to stand beside Henry and tried not to fidget as they waited for the guests to arrive.

"It's a fine piece of land," a man's booming voice could be heard saying, "if you're willing to stay and work yourself to the bone. As for myself, I'm itching to get to California and see some of that gold with my very own eyes."

Caroline felt Henry twitch beside her. She turned to look at him, and he grinned back. "Gold!" he whispered.

"And there's no stopping Mr. Hale when he has a notion in his head," the lady's voice said laughingly.

"Here we are," Mr. Holbrook's voice announced, and then suddenly the small room was full of people. Mr. Holbrook made the introductions.

"My, what fine, strong-looking boys." Mr. Hale bellowed, shaking hands with Joseph, Henry, and Thomas each in turn. Then he bowed to Caroline and her sisters. "And what pretty little ladies." He turned to look at Mother, and his bushy white eyebrows flew up. "Are all these children yours, ma'am?" he asked in wonder, and Mother nodded and answered that they were.

Mrs. Hale took Mother's hand in her own and patted it. "You must call me Delight," she said in a warm voice. "It's so nice to meet you, my dear, and your lovely family."

Caroline had never heard of anyone named

Delight. It was a pretty name, and it fit Mrs. Hale perfectly. Her cheeks were pink and rosy like apples. Her bright eyes looked around the little cabin with interest, and the pleasant smile never left her face.

"What a cozy home," she said.

Mr. Hale was just as jolly as his wife. With his large belly and white whiskers, Caroline thought he looked exactly like Santeclaus. He laughed a great deal, and his laughter was catching. After a few minutes Caroline felt like laughing too. Even Mr. Holbrook's lips were turned up in a smile.

"Well then," Mr. Hale said, clapping his hands together. "Are we all present now, Mrs. Quiner?" He turned his head to and fro. "No more children to come running out of the woodwork?"

Mother blushed a little and shook her head.

"Then I think it's best we get started," Mr. Hale announced.

"What a lovely day for a wedding," Mrs. Hale said, taking Mother's hand again. "As they say, 'Wednesday best day of all.'"

Mother's eyes were shining and she nodded her head. Caroline wanted to ask what Mrs. Hale meant about Wednesday, but there wasn't time. Mr. Hale placed Mother and Mr. Holbrook side by side before the hearth and told the children to gather round. He took out a pair of half-moon glasses from his vest and a small Bible from his coat pocket. He read a few verses; then he took Mother's and Mr. Holbrook's hands and put them together over the open pages.

In a solemn voice he said, "In full view of these witnesses and the Lord Almighty, I now pronounce you man and wife."

Mother glanced up at Mr. Holbrook with a shy smile. Mr. Holbrook gave a nod, his blue eyes sparkling a little, then looked down at his boots. No one knew what to say.

Mr. Hale clapped his hands together and laughed heartily. Mrs. Hale rushed to Mother and kissed her on the cheek.

"A long and happy life, my dear," she said.

There was laughter again as Mother and the girls scurried to set the food on the table.

Everyone talked and ate at once. The little room buzzed with voices. Mr. Hale told them how he and Mrs. Hale had come to Wisconsin many years ago and bought up pieces of land all around Concord, including the stretch that ran from the Territorial Road to their farm.

"So we're neighbors then?" Joseph asked in surprise.

"Not for long, my boy," Mr. Hale said, wiping his whiskers neatly with the linen napkin and patting his wife's hand on the table. "We're headed out west before I'm too old. I'm bound and determined to get my hands on some of that gold."

"I want to get some gold, too," Henry said in a loud voice. "I wish I could head out with you."

Mother looked at him sharply. "Henry!" she scolded.

Henry frowned and ducked his head, but Mr. Hale's hearty laugh rang out. "That's a boy itching for adventure. I was just the same at his age." He gave Henry a wink. "I'd take you with me, my boy. The good Lord knows

I could use a young able body like yourself. But I reckon you're needed around here."

Henry turned to Mother excitedly. "Just think! If I went out west and found gold, I could bring it back and we wouldn't have to work so hard."

"A pound of pluck is worth a ton of luck," Mr. Holbrook said sternly, and again Henry's eyes fell to his plate.

No one quite knew what to say, but once more Mr. Hale's cheerfulness eased any tension at the table. "'Tis true enough there's a good deal of risk involved in leaving hearth and home and staking your life on a claim of gold. But all my life I've been a lucky man. I hope my luck will hold out." Then he spoke to Henry again. "Wait a few more years, young lad. From what I hear, there's plenty of gold out there for everyone."

Joseph began to ask questions about California, and Mr. Hale answered each in turn. Caroline noticed Henry's eyes growing bright again, and he seemed more excited than she had ever seen him. She suddenly remembered

Reverend Speakes' words about the sinfulness of greed, and it made her shudder to remember how scared she had been at Camp Meeting.

"Won't it be a difficult journey?" Mother asked, turning to Mrs. Hale.

"I knew when I married Mr. Hale that there would be no sitting around collecting dust," she said, smiling her rosy smile. "I've heard California is quite beautiful, and the weather is always fair."

"I wager it will beat a Wisconsin winter any day." Mr. Hale slapped his hand on the table.

"But what will you do with your land here?" Joseph asked.

Mr. Hale's bushy eyebrows shot up. "Why, I'm aiming to sell some of it to your pa," he cried. "We'll sign the papers this very afternoon."

For a moment Caroline felt confused. Her father was dead, so how could he sign papers? Then she realized Mr. Hale meant Mr. Holbrook, her new pa. Her mind swirled with

thoughts of Father and Brookfield and candlesticks.

At the end of the table Mr. Holbrook cleared
his throat. "Mr. Hale has been most generous in his dealings," he said. "Combined with
Charlotte's land, our farm will now run all the
way down to the Territorial Road."

Caroline could hardly believe it. She thought
of all that land and all those trees. Caroline
could tell Henry was thinking, too, of the trees
that would have to be felled before the land
could be planted. His eyes, shining when
speaking of the gold, had dimmed.

But then Mother set the blueberry cake on
the table, and Caroline turned her attention
to eating every last bite of the sweet tangy
treat.

When the cake was all gone, Caroline suddenly remembered what Mrs. Hale had said
before. In a quiet moment she asked, "Excuse me, ma'am—what did you mean about
Wednesday being best?"

Mrs. Hale's eyes lit up. "Why it's an old
wedding saying about what day of the week

to get married. Haven't you ever heard it, my dear?" When Caroline shook her head, Mrs. Hale began to recite:

"Monday for wealth,
Tuesday for health,
Wednesday best day of all,
Thursday for losses,
Friday for crosses,
Saturday no luck at all."

Mrs. Hale reached out to pat Caroline's hand. "Now, what do you think of that?"

"I'm glad you didn't come on Thursday, Friday, or Saturday!" Caroline exclaimed, and everyone laughed.

It was so merry inside the little cabin, Caroline wished the Hales would never leave. She wished that she had known them while they were still neighbors. But they would be on their way to California by the end of the week, and had to leave the little cabin to prepare for their journey.

"Perhaps we'll meet again," Mr. Hale said

in his jolly voice as he shook Mother's hand. Mrs. Hale gave them each a small hug before following her husband out the door. For a while Caroline could still hear Mr. Hale's booming voice as they walked back through the woods, with the boys and Mr. Holbrook to escort them. Caroline knew Henry would be using every spare moment to ask more about gold.

With everyone gone, the cabin suddenly seemed very quiet and empty. Mother let out a little sigh.

"So much excitement over the past few days!" she exclaimed. "It will be good to get back to our everyday routine."

Caroline nodded, but inside she wished all the fun could go on a little longer. She watched Mother carefully as she busied herself at the cookstove. It was strange to think that she had been married only a few short hours ago.

"Mother?" Caroline asked in a timid voice.

"Yes, Caroline?" Mother waited, her eyes tired but smiling.

"What should we call Mr. Holbrook now?" Caroline asked.

Mother thought for a moment before she answered. "I think you'll need to ask him that yourself."

Silently Caroline went back to wiping the dishes. It was hard to think of Mr. Holbrook as anything but Mr. Holbrook.

When he returned late that afternoon, Mr. Holbrook carried a large leather satchel and his long rifle. Now there would be two guns hanging above the door. He also brought something wrapped in burlap, which he handed to Mother.

She opened the package. It was a little wooden shelf he had carved.

"Thank you, Frederick," Mother said softly as she put the shelf on the table. Caroline and Martha and Eliza gathered round. It was not so fine a gift as silver candlesticks, but there were two pretty roses carved along the sides of the shelf, and the wood was velvety smooth to touch. Mr. Holbrook hung the little shelf near the dish dresser, and Mother put the tin cups on it.

Then Mr. Holbrook went into the small bedroom. Caroline and her sisters stood in the doorway watching as he hammered wooden pegs into the walls opposite each other. When he was finished, he strung a long piece of rope between the beds. Then he hung a quilt over the rope. Now the room was divided into two rooms.

In the girls' room there were one quilt wall and three log walls. On one side was the door to the big room and on the other was the chest where they kept their clothes, and above the bed was the little window. Caroline was glad that her side of the room got the window.

After such a lively dinner, supper seemed especially quiet. As the dark pressed against the glass windowpanes, Caroline kept expecting Mr. Holbrook to put on his hat and give his nod and head out into the night. But with a start she realized he would not be leaving.

He settled in a chair by the open door and filled his pipe. The rich, tangy smell of tobacco filled the air. The boys played checkers in the corner. Henry did not whoop and holler as he generally did when he skipped over Joseph's chips. Thomas watched with saucer eyes as Mr. Holbrook began to whittle at a piece of kindling. He edged closer but did not ask if it was a wooden man Mr. Holbrook was making.

Mother sat in her rocker as usual, her needle flashing as she did her mending. She stopped every now and then to help Eliza with her sampler. Martha and Caroline sat together at the table, working on their quilts.

Caroline wanted to ask Mr. Holbrook what they should call him, but she did not have the courage. Neither did Martha. She shrugged her shoulders when Caroline nudged her, and then they both bowed their heads back over their quilt patches.

Caroline tried to concentrate on her sewing, but she could not make her stitches small and even no matter how hard she tried. She couldn't help glancing around the room every few minutes. Everything felt different inside the little cabin, but she decided it wasn't a bad feeling at all.

A New Pa

E ven though Mr. Holbrook had eaten
breakfast with them before, when he
worked for Mr. Kellogg, Caroline wondered what it would be like to sit with him
at the head of the table first thing in the morning. But she did not have the chance to find
out. Long before the light had peeked through
the trees, Mr. Holbrook and the boys left the
cabin to begin their day's work clearing the
new land.

Mother fixed bowls of mush for the girls'
breakfast. She explained that the boys had

already eaten and would not be seen again until dinnertime.

The clearing seemed very quiet to Caroline as she went to the shed to fetch the water and grain for the geese and hens. It was hard to believe so much had changed in one day. She almost wished Henry would leap out from behind the henhouse and scare her as he often did.

As usual, Joseph had left two buckets of fresh water from the river beside the shed. Caroline opened the door and pulled up the heavy lid to the wooden box where the grain was stored. She filled two empty buckets and set one aside. She carried one bucket of grain and one bucket of water toward the pen, where the geese were already honking and flapping about. As soon as they caught sight of her, the geese rushed for the fence, a brown-and-white whirl of feathers.

Caroline did not go into the pen. Geese were pretty to look at, but they were not very nice. If you were not careful, they nipped at you with their big beaks, and they fought among themselves for each little bit of grain. Caroline dug her hands into the bucket and tossed handfuls of feed over the fence. Once more there was a great show of honking and fluttering. Caroline took the old broom handle she kept beside the fence and nudged at the bigger birds.

"You save some of that for your babies," she scolded, pushing the bigger birds into one corner and throwing in more grain. The smaller gray goslings scampered about, pecking at the ground. "Come September you all need to be as fat as can be," she added, then stood back, satisfied that all the geese were getting a fair share.

While the geese were busy with the feed, Caroline carried the water bucket to the gate at the opposite end of the pen. She opened it just enough to pour the fresh water into the trough, then secured the gate again.

Caroline stood watching the geese for a while longer to give herself a rest. Mother had given Mr. Kellogg the money for the geese, and he had brought them back last spring from a trip to Watertown. There had been only a handful of geese then. Now there were twice as many, and there would be more come fall. Then they would sell the plump birds at the market and with the money buy stores for the winter.

Caring for the chickens had always been Caroline's special chore, and she loved it. But the geese made the morning a little harder. Martha had offered to help when Mother had first bought them, but Caroline had said no.

Caroline went back to the shed and exchanged the empty buckets for the full ones. At the henhouse she opened the little door, and the hens came flapping out, clucking and searching for grain.

"Wait a minute." Caroline laughed, reaching into the bucket and tossing the feed across the ground. As soon as the hens were contentedly pecking at the feed, Caroline took up her egg basket and went into the henhouse. She checked all the little nesting boxes Mr. Holbrook had helped build. She found four eggs, which she carefully tucked into her basket filled with soft grass. She noticed that the leaves and grass along the ground were still a little damp from Sunday's rain. In all the excitement Caroline had forgotten about the henhouse floor. Chickens did not like wet feet, so Caroline knew she would need to rake out the old leaves and put in fresh ones.

Caroline took the eggs to Mother and explained about the wet leaves.

"Take Eliza with you," Mother said. It was a hard job for one person to do alone.

Together Eliza and Caroline raked out the henhouse. With Wolf following close, they went into the woods.

"We still don't know what to call Mr. Holbrook," Eliza said, as they gathered up dry grasses and fallen leaves in their aprons.

"I suppose we have plenty of time to figure it out," Caroline said matter-of-factly.

"Do you like Mr. Holbrook?" Eliza asked.

Caroline thought for a moment. "Yes," she said. "I do."

"Henry doesn't seem to," Eliza said.

Caroline nodded slowly.

"Why?" Eliza persisted.

"I don't know," Caroline admitted. "I don't think he likes being told what to do."

"But Mother tells him what to do," Eliza said.

"That's different," Caroline reasoned. "Mr. Holbrook is somebody new."

When they had as many grasses and leaves as their aprons could hold, they headed back to the henhouse. They shook out their skirts and raked the grass and leaves evenly across the dirt floor.

"There, now your squawkers will be happy," Eliza said.

At dinnertime Mr. Holbrook and the boys came trudging back through the woods. The boys looked more tired than usual. Even little Thomas walked with slumped shoulders, but when he saw his sisters, he perked up.

"I made big piles of brush!" he announced, and Mr. Holbrook patted him on the shoulder.

"A good little worker," he said with a nod of his head.

Henry was silent. Caroline noticed a deep gash on his hand.

"It's nothing," Henry mumbled, but Mother led him to the washbasin to wash the cut in soap and water. She rubbed some comfrey root over it to prevent infection, then tied a clean rag from her rag basket around his hand.

"Young Henry needs to keep his thoughts on his work," Mr. Holbrook said. "Cutting timber is not child's play."

Henry scowled down at his hand but said nothing. Caroline felt a band tighten across her chest. She hoped Henry would be more careful in the woods.

At the table Caroline felt shy with Mr. Holbrook there. She thought that Martha and Eliza did too. But Joseph talked excitedly about the new land Mr. Holbrook had bought from Mr. Hale.

"It's a good stretch," he said. "Full of trees, of course, but the earth is dark and rich."

"Another week of clearing and tilling, and I expect we'll be ready to do some planting," Mr. Holbrook said.

"Not by a jugful!" Henry sputtered. "It's too late! Mr. Ben always said to plant early if you want a cellar full of stores 'fore winter's first blast."

"Your manners, Henry," Mother said sharply. Then she explained to Mr. Holbrook about the Carpenters and how they had helped in the past.

Mr. Holbrook nodded. "Perhaps I'll have the good fortune to meet them one of these days."

"I hope so!" Martha blurted out, and then she looked down, her cheeks flushing pink. Caroline knew she was thinking about Charlie.

Mr. Holbrook cleared his throat. "I reckon it does appear foolish to seed the land this late. But the way I figure it, there's a good chance the seeds will take and we'll have a longer harvest. Even if we do lose some crops to an early frost, we'll be certain to have a better harvest come next year when the ground is used to growing."

"Whatever you think best, Frederick," Mother said.

Caroline saw how Henry's eyes flashed, and she was glad Mr. Holbrook did not seem to notice.

Mr. Holbrook sipped at his coffee thoughtfully. "With all the trees we're clearing, there'll be enough to build a barn come spring," Mr. Holbrook said. "Life will be all the more pleasant once we've a few animals roaming the land."

Thomas dropped his spoon in his bowl and clapped his hands together. "Will we have horses?" he asked.

"Well, first I think we should get a pair of oxen," Mr. Holbrook answered. "The clearing and planting would go much faster if we had a team of good, strong oxen."

"We'll need a pig." Henry spoke grudgingly. In Brookfield they had always had a pig, and it was Henry's job to take care of it.

Mr. Holbrook nodded his head without taking notice of Henry's tone. "And don't forget a cow or two," he said.

"We'll have butter!" Eliza exclaimed.

"And milk!" Thomas added.

"And salt pork!" Martha laughed.

Even Mother smiled. "A whole cellarful of stores would be such a blessing," she said brightly.

Caroline thought about all the winters they had spent with little to get them through. Once when they were nearly starving, two Indians had brought them a whole deer. Caroline's mouth watered as she remembered how the meat had smoked over the fire for days and days, until it was tender and ready to eat.

"And as soon as we have a barn, I'd like to start laying the foundation for a frame house," Mr. Holbrook announced. "There's scarcely room in this cabin for all of us now. Why, in no time at all Thomas will be near a grown man, with his head rubbing the rafters."

Thomas patted his head and opened his eyes wide. "I'll be that big?"

Everyone around the table laughed. Caroline did not feel so shy anymore.

"Well, no use sitting around chattering like chipmunks," Mr. Holbrook said, pushing up from his chair. "Talk never put food on the table. It's back to work, boys, or it will be a coon's age 'fore we have all the fine things we're dreaming of."

As soon as Mr. Holbrook and the boys were gone, Eliza rushed up to Caroline.

"He *will* build us a frame house just like our old one," she exclaimed. "I knew he would!"

As Caroline began to clear the table, she let herself imagine what it would be like to have two whole floors, as they had in Brookfield. There would be a room for Mother and Mr. Holbrook, a room for the boys, and a room for the girls. There might even be an extra room in case Grandma came to live with them again.

"Do you think we should help the boys?" Caroline asked Mother. Even though she had not liked dragging the trees and brush into piles last year, she suddenly wanted to help all she could. The more hands, the quicker they would have fields of crops and a barn and animals and a new house.

"There's plenty of work to do around here," Mother said firmly.

Thursday was generally the day to do the churning. But they already had butter from the wedding, so now they did the mending instead. Mother put the pile of clothes on the table and sorted through them. Caroline was used to sewing up the little tears and rips in the boys' clothing, but now there was an extra set of work shirts and trousers to mend. Mother gave Caroline one of Mr. Holbrook's shirts, and she began to make little stitches along a torn place on the cuff. As she worked, Caroline suddenly wondered where Mr. Holbrook was from. She had never thought to ask.

"Did Mr. Holbrook come from back east like you?" Caroline blurted.

"Yes, but not from Boston," Mother answered without looking up from her needle. "His family lived in Connecticut."

"Where is his family now?" Martha asked.

"He only has one sister left, and she lives far away in Chicago," Mother answered.

Caroline finished her mending and rubbed her fingers along the rough handwoven fabric. She knew that Mr. Holbrook was not rich and did not wear fine boughten clothes like Mr. Kellogg, but he kept his shirts and trousers neat. The tear on the cuff was the only place that needed to be mended.

In the middle of the afternoon Mother said the girls could take a jug of water to where the boys were working. Then they could pick some greens and wild strawberries for supper on their way home. Martha carried the heavy jug while Caroline and Eliza swung the empty baskets as they walked through the shady woods. Wolf went bounding ahead, chasing after rabbits and squirrels.

Long before she could see the boys through the trees, Caroline heard the sound of axes ringing. The sharp smell of burning wood tickled her nose, and a wisp of smoke hung in the air. Mr. Holbrook was burning the brush piles Thomas had built.

Caroline heard Henry's voice call out, "Howdy Wolf, what are you doing here?" Then she saw his grinning face as he caught sight of the girls with the jug.

"My throat's as dry as a sack of ash," he

said, reaching for the jug and taking big gulps.

"Be sure to save enough for us," Joseph chided, swinging his ax to the ground.

The boys' shirts were dark with sweat. Thomas took Caroline's and Martha's hands and showed them the smoldering stacks he had made.

"Two whole piles!" he yelled, and Caroline complimented him, but deep down she was disappointed. There was only a little patch of open ground. Gazing through the thick growth of trees, she feared all the plans from dinner were very far away. There were so many more trees to clear, Caroline did not see how they could have them all chopped down by winter.

Mr. Holbrook must have noticed her disappointment, because he said stoutly, "It may not look like much just yet, but there'll be a barn come spring and a house next fall, I promise you." He sounded so sure that Caroline believed him.

After Mr. Holbrook had turned away, Caroline

glanced at Henry. He was rubbing the hand Mother had bandaged.

"You know where I'd like to be right now, Caroline?" he said under his breath.

Caroline nodded her head. "Fishing."

"Nope," he said. "I'd like to be on the trail to California. Not cutting down any old trees."

Caroline looked off in the direction Henry was gazing, but she could not imagine wanting to go on such a journey. It had seemed like a long trip from Brookfield to Concord last year, but that had taken only three days. She couldn't imagine going all the way to California. Mr. Hale had said it would take several months to cross the whole west by wagon.

"The afternoon's a-wasting," Mr. Holbrook said after he had taken a few swigs of water. He smiled at Caroline as he handed her the jug. "Thank you kindly, ladies, for bringing the water."

On the way home the girls stopped to pick the little ripe strawberries that grew in patches along the forest floor. Near the river they looked for the bright-yellow flowers called marsh marigolds. The leaves were good to eat. When their baskets were full, they headed home. Mother was pleased with what they had gathered. She put some strawberries aside for preserves, but the rest she made into a pie. Then she made a pot of marigold greens for supper. There was hot bean soup and johnny-cake as well. By the time Mr. Holbrook and the boys came home, the little house was filled with good rich smells.

"One thing's for certain," Mr. Holbrook said at the end of the meal. "A man could never go hungry with your mother around."

Caroline couldn't agree more. Even when there was little food to eat, Mother always managed to make things taste good.

As night fell, Caroline thought about how a whole day had passed with Mr. Holbrook living there among them. She waited until he was settled in a chair with his pipe and his whittling. Then she crossed the room and stood before him.

"Excuse me, sir?" she asked hesitantly.

Mr. Holbrook stopped his whittling and looked up at her in surprise.

"What is it, Caroline?" he asked, taking the pipe out of his mouth.

"What should we call you now?" Her voice sounded very small to her ears.

Mr. Holbrook's eyes looked startled for a moment. He reached up and scratched at his beard. He glanced around the room. Everyone was watching and waiting.

"Well, I'd be honored if you called me Pa," he said, and his voice seemed choked a little in his throat.

Caroline nodded and went back to sit beside Martha at the table. As she passed the checkerboard, she saw the hard, sullen look on Henry's face. It made her feel jumbled up inside. Henry was her brother, and she loved him more than anything, but sometimes he could be very pigheaded.

Caroline settled in beside Martha and carefully worked at her quilt. Outside, there were the nearby sounds of the nighthawks darting to and fro in the clearing and the hoot owl *whoo-whoo*ing from its hollow tree and the cicadas humming in the leaves. Far off in the distance a lone wolf gave its lonely call. Inside, there were only the sounds of the checkers clacking on the checkerboard and Mr. Holbrook's knife scraping gently against wood. As she worked in the cozy quiet, Caroline thought about the new name and smiled to herself. Mr. Holbrook could not take the place of Father, but she was happy that he was her pa.

The Bee Skep

By early July half an acre of land had been cleared and turned. Now it was time to plant it with more corn and potatoes and pumpkins and turnips. All one morning and afternoon the family worked together in the hot sun, dropping seeds into the rich soil. Caroline and Eliza and Thomas chanted as they walked along the rows:

"One for the blackbird, one for the crow,
One for the squirrel, and two to grow."

Martha said she was too old to sing along.

"But how do you remember how many seeds to put down?" Eliza asked.

"I'm old enough to remember without singing that baby chant," Martha answered.

Caroline felt like saying something smart back, but she knew Mother would scold her. It seemed to her that both Martha and Henry acted strangely now that they were getting older.

At the end of the day, Caroline's skin itched from the dust and sweat, and her back ached from bending over, but she was pleased when Mr. Holbrook gave his nod of approval.

"That takes care of this year's crops," Mr. Holbrook said. "But me and the boys have still got a ways to go 'fore we have this land tamed for next year's planting."

Henry let out a disapproving sound through his lips, but Mr. Holbrook and Mother did not seem to notice. Joseph grinned and reached out to tug on Caroline's braid.

"We'll have a barnyard full of animals yet," he said, winking at her.

Caroline took a final look at the new garden before she followed Mother into the house. She hoped with all her might that the vegetables would have time to grow before the first frost.

The next day Mr. Holbrook lingered over dinner longer than usual. He glanced at Caroline as he said, "Me and the boys came by Caroline's bee tree as we were clearing last week. Seems to me we plumb forgot about making that bee skep."

Caroline smiled. In April she had seen a line of bees flying in and out of a hole in an old hollow tree. Henry had said that meant the tree was full of honey, and he had helped Caroline mark the tree with a rag from Mother's rag basket so that they could find it again. Mr. Holbrook had said he would help them build a bee skep, but with all the work no one had even thought about the bees for a long time.

"I've a notion to have some honey with your mother's good bread," Mr. Holbrook said. "I'm aiming to make the skep this very afternoon."

"May I help, Pa?" Caroline asked. It still felt strange to call him Pa even though she had been doing it for weeks now. In her mind she still thought of him as Mr. Holbrook.

"You'd best ask your mother," Mr. Holbrook answered.

Mother looked uncertain. It was Friday, which meant it was the day to clean the whole house.

"Oh, please, Mother?" Caroline begged.

"I suppose so," Mother said finally.

"Thank you, Mother!" Caroline smiled at Henry. She expected him to be just as excited as she was. She knew how much he loved fresh honey, and he had been happy when Mr. Holbrook had first suggested that they begin to farm their own bees. But Henry only gulped down the rest of his food without smiling back.

"All right then," Mr. Holbrook said to Caroline. "The first thing you can do is find some good thick thread."

"A needle too?" Caroline asked, but Mr. Holbrook shook his head.

"No," he answered. "That won't be big enough. I'll fashion a kind of needle out of a blackberry bramble."

Caroline quickly helped clear the table while Mother got some thick brown thread from her sewing basket.

"Make sure to keep your bonnet on," Mother called as Caroline rushed out the door with the thread. "The sun's awfully hot today."

Mr. Holbrook and Thomas were waiting for her beside the shed, holding two empty baskets and a bucket.

"Pa said I could help too," Thomas announced, grinning up at Mr. Holbrook. Caroline reached out and tousled her brother's golden curls.

"All right then," Mr. Holbrook said. "Since we won't be seeing any wild hay 'fore August, we'll head down to the river. Sweet grass and cattails should do just fine."

Caroline was surprised. "I thought a skep was made of wood," she said.

Mr. Holbrook shook his head. "A skep is like a big upside-down basket," he explained as they headed through the woods, Wolf dashing ahead of them. "Straw is best for skep making, but the grass is tall and thick enough this time of year to be a good substitute."

The rippling water was cool against her feet and ankles as Caroline walked along the bank, gathering the tall grasses and cattails. Thomas followed behind, also pulling up big handfuls. Mr. Holbrook went to the blackberry bushes and cut a bramble with the sharp knife he wore at his belt.

When they had two baskets full of grass, Mr. Holbrook dipped a large bucket full of water, and they headed back to the clearing. Under the shade of a big pine tree they spread out the grasses and cattails. Mr. Holbrook quickly cut off the heads of the cattails. He poured the water from the bucket into a trough. Then he told Caroline and Thomas to put all the grasses and cattail stems into the water to soak.

While they waited, Mr. Holbrook began to

whittle on the blackberry bramble. Caroline and Thomas watched as he made a sharp point on one end and a hole through the bramble on the other end. It looked just like a sewing needle, only bigger. Then he took the thick thread from Caroline and threaded it through and knotted it.

"Reckon we're ready to start coiling," he said, placing a stool beside the trough. "Now watch what I do, and then I'll let you try it." Slowly he twisted several stalks of the grass and cattails together, making a good, strong rope as thick as Caroline's wrist. This he made into a ring, twisting the ends tightly together.

"That's the bottom of the skep," he said. Then he started all over again. Only this ring was a little smaller than the first. He sewed the two rings together with the blackberry needle and thread.

The skep grew taller and taller, with each new ring smaller than the one below it.

"Here, now you try," Mr. Holbrook said, holding out a shock of grass.

Caroline took the wet grass in her hands

and tried to twist it into a rope as Mr. Holbrook
had done, but the tough blades kept slipping
out of her fingers. Mr. Holbrook placed his
hands over hers and showed her how to work
quickly so the strands would not come undone.
His hands were rough and callused from all
the work he did, but they were strong and
gentle at the same time.

"It takes practice is all," Mr. Holbrook said,
letting go so Caroline could try it by herself
again.

"Did you learn to make a skep when you
were a boy like me?" Thomas asked.

Mr. Holbrook shook his head. "No sir," he
answered. "We never tried to keep bees when
I was growing up. But we did like to have wild
honey. My pa always spent a lot of time searching out bee trees. Sometimes we'd stumble on
one like Caroline did, by following the bees."
He nodded at her. "But most times it was just
pure luck."

"Like Mr. Hale searching for his gold?"
Caroline asked.

"Searching for bee's gold is a mite different

from searching for fool's gold," Mr. Holbrook said. He helped Caroline sew the ring to the skep and start twisting another rope.

"How did you learn to make a skep, then?" Caroline asked.

"Some Indians taught me," Mr. Holbrook answered.

"Indians?" Thomas' eyes were round. "Mother is afraid of Indians."

"Like all folks in this world, there's good Indians and there's bad Indians," Mr. Holbrook said. "But I myself have never run into the bad kind."

"Are there Indians around here?" Thomas asked.

"Used to be all kinds of tribes here," Mr. Holbrook answered. "Potawatomi and Winnebago and Menominee. Now most of them have been run off. When I first came to this territory, I was barely Henry's age. And I was Joseph's age when my folks died and I was the only one left to take care of my little sister. If it hadn't been for some Winnebago teaching us how to survive, me and Lucy surely would have perished."

Caroline told Mr. Holbrook about the Indians who had helped them by giving them meat during the hard winter in Brookfield.

"Just like I said, there's good and bad folk everywhere," Mr. Holbrook said as he began to coil the next rope smaller than the last. Caroline watched as the ropes circled smaller and smaller until they made a rounded top.

The skep was nearly as tall as Thomas when Mr. Holbrook said, "That'll do," and set the skep on the ground. They all stepped back.

"It looks like a funny hat," Thomas said. And it was true. The skep looked like a man's very tall hat except it had no brim.

Mr. Holbrook began to go over the whole skep once again with the blackberry needle and Mother's thread. "It needs to be nice and tight so it doesn't come apart in the rain," he explained.

"How will we get the bees inside?" Caroline asked.

"We'll worry about that tomorrow," Mr.

Holbrook answered. "Bees are all riled up in the afternoon. We'll get them into the skep at first light, when they're still sleepy."

When Mr. Holbrook was sure the skep was solid, he set it in a warm spot in the clearing so that the sun would bake the wet grass and make it stronger.

"Now we'll build a platform to hold the skep once the bees are inside," Mr. Holbrook said. "Bees don't like to be on the cold ground."

Caroline and Thomas followed Mr. Holbrook to the woodpile. With his ax he split some logs and cut them into square pieces. Thomas helped him by holding nails, and in no time Mr. Holbrook had built a little square box.

"We'd best get back to our chores now," Mr. Holbrook said. "First thing in the morning, we'll see how the bees take to the skep."

That night Mother looked through her rag basket and found a square piece of very thin muslin. She cut and sewed until she had made a kind of hood for Mr. Holbrook to wear over his hat, covering his face and neck.

"This way the bees won't sting me when I come to take some of their honeycomb," Mr. Holbrook explained.

Caroline put the hood over her head and looked around the cabin. She could see a little through the filmy material. Joseph asked about the skep and keeping bees, and Martha and Eliza and Thomas sat around listening as Mr. Holbrook spoke. Only Henry sat by himself, whittling at a piece of wood.

In the morning, when the room was still dark, Caroline heard a creaking in the bed that was on the other side of the quilt wall. Mr. Holbrook was getting up. Caroline waited until he had pulled on his boots and walked into the big room, and then she jumped out of bed too.

"You're in an awful hurry this morning," Martha said sleepily.

"I'm going with Pa," Caroline answered, wriggling into her dress and apron.

"Well, you better hope those bees don't come after you," Martha said.

Mother had already put the mush on the

table. Caroline sat down with the boys and ate her breakfast. Then she followed Mr. Holbrook and Thomas out the door into the gray morning light. Henry and Joseph swung their axes over their shoulders and headed off in the opposite direction.

"Don't you want to watch the bees?" Caroline called.

Henry shrugged, but Joseph turned and called back, "Too much chopping to do. You can tell us all about it at dinner."

Mr. Holbrook brought one empty bucket and a tin cup from the house and gave them to Caroline. He gave another empty bucket to Thomas. He picked up the skep, and together they headed into the woods. Caroline told Wolf to stay. Mr. Holbrook said Wolf might make the bees mad with his barking.

At the river Mr. Holbrook scooped some black, sticky mud into Thomas' bucket. Then they walked between the trees until they found the one Caroline and Henry had marked with a long red rag. It was a big hollow tree, and it had a hole in the trunk that Caroline knew was the entrance to the hive. The rag was still on the tree, blowing a little in the morning breeze. Caroline saw one or two bees buzzing around. Mr. Holbrook stopped at a good distance and set the skep down.

"Now I want you young'uns to stay here and don't move an inch," Mr. Holbrook said. "Even though it's morning and they're less ornery now, bees don't much like sharing their honey."

Caroline watched as Mr. Holbrook pulled his leather work gloves out of his pocket and put them on, making sure that the gloves overlapped the cuffs of his shirt sleeves. Then he put the muslin hood over his hat. He knelt down and took handfuls of mud from the bucket and rubbed it along the inside of the skep.

When he was finished, he walked on silent feet to the bee tree. Taking his knife from his belt, Mr. Holbrook reached into the huge hole in the trunk. Caroline held her breath as bees buzzed around him, landing on his shirt and hood. After a little while Mr. Holbrook's gloved hand appeared again. He was holding a thick, sticky comb. He knelt down and pushed it into the mud inside the skep. Then he reached into the tree again and brought out another comb, and another, and another.

Caroline felt her insides begin to quiver. There were so many bees on Mr. Holbrook now that parts of his hood and all of his gloves were black. As soon as the combs were secure, Mr. Holbrook knelt down, and suddenly, like magic, all the bees on Mr. Holbrook flew into the skep. Caroline felt like clapping, but she knew she shouldn't make a peep. Beside her, Thomas was bouncing silently up and down on his toes.

Mr. Holbrook stood up, took out the tin cup, and reached again into the bee tree. He filled the cup again and again, dumping golden honey into the clean bucket. A few bees buzzed angrily in the air, but then they flew back into the tree. Finally Mr. Holbrook carried both buckets back to Caroline and Thomas.

"You two walk on ahead," he said. "I'll follow with the skep." But first he held out his knife. Two small chunks of honeycomb were wedged on the end. Thomas reached for one chunk and Caroline took the other, but they weren't sure what to do with it.

"Haven't you ever tasted honeycomb?" Mr. Holbrook asked. He seemed to chuckle a little, but Caroline wasn't sure because she couldn't see his face behind the hood. "It's good to suck on," he said. Caroline and Thomas slowly put the pieces into their mouths. The sweet flavor of honey burst in Caroline's mouth. She and Thomas looked at each other and grinned. All the way home the flavor lingered. It was better than penny candy from the general store. When all the honey was gone, Mr. Holbrook told them to throw away the soft wax from the comb.

Back in the clearing Thomas went running toward the house, shouting at the top of his lungs, "We've got bees! We've got honey!"

Mother came to the door, wiping her hands on her apron. Martha and Eliza ran outside, looking at Mr. Holbrook and the skep with big eyes. Gently Mr. Holbrook placed the skep on the platform he had built. He propped it up on one end with a thin wedge of wood so the bees could go in and out.

"In a few days we'll see if the bees take to their new home," he said, taking off his gloves and turning toward Mother. "In the meantime I've brought you some fresh honey, Charlotte."

"What a treat," Mother cried, taking the heavy bucket from Caroline.

Mr. Holbrook nodded, then squinted up at the blue patch of sky. "Well, the day's a-wasting." He swung his ax over his shoulder and headed off in the direction the boys had gone that morning, Thomas following at his heels.

All that week Mr. Holbrook watched the skep. In the mornings he lifted the basket carefully and peered at the bees, who were busy going in and out of the combs, making honey. He let Caroline and Thomas look, too. The bees seemed happy in their new home. By the end of the week, Mr. Holbrook declared that the bees would stay in the skep.

"When will we have more honey?" Caroline asked.

"Come fall we'll have a good supply," Mr. Holbrook answered. "Then we'll make another skep so we'll have even more honey next year."

Caroline smiled to think of having honey all year round to drizzle on their mush in the morning and to spread on their bread at dinner and at supper, too.

Wedding Gifts

One Saturday, after the baking was done, Mother and the girls went out to the garden to grub the stumps. This garden was not like their garden in Brookfield. Even with all the trees cut down, there were still stumps sticking up here and there among the rows of vegetables and herbs. Once a week they had to take grub hoes and hack at the little tree shoots that grew up around the stumps. Otherwise there would be more trees for the boys to clear next year.

The sun was burning down overhead, and

Caroline had to stop every now and then to wipe her face with her apron. She was glad she had a bonnet on, because it gave her a little shade from the fierce light. She could hear the ringing of the boys' axes in the distance, and she could smell the smoke from the bonfires. Mother sang as she worked, but Caroline felt too hot to join her. The air was always sticky and thick now. Even Wolf did not like to run and bark very much. He lay in the shade, switching his tail and snapping at flies.

"What beautiful singing," a deep voice said. "I thought it was an angel leading us through the woods."

Caroline nearly dropped her hoe as she whirled around. Wolf jumped up to growl but settled down again when Mother spoke sharply to him.

Mr. Kellogg was there at the edge of the clearing. Mrs. Kellogg was also there, on a great chestnut mare, and Margaret was beside her on a small spotted pony.

"Good afternoon." Mr. Kellogg spoke again.

"I hope we didn't startle you."

Caroline suddenly wished she could melt into the ground. She loved having visitors, but not when she was so dirty from working in the garden. She could tell Mother felt the same way. Mother daintily wiped her brow with her apron and touched her hands to her hair.

"Why, Mr. and Mrs. Kellogg, what a surprise," she said politely, walking between the garden rows toward them. "What brings you out on such a warm day?"

"Forgive us for coming without notice," Mr. Kellogg said. "But I've only just returned to Concord and learned of your marriage. Laura insisted we come right away to give you our best wishes." Mr. Kellogg stepped forward, and Caroline now noticed that he carried a wooden crate and was leading a pretty brown calf by a leather strap.

"Why, how very kind of you," Mother said, her face full of surprise. "Won't you please come in out of the sun and rest awhile?"

"We don't mean to trouble you," Mrs. Kellogg said sweetly. But Mother insisted.

As Mrs. Kellogg guided her handsome horse toward the cabin, Caroline again thought she looked like a beautiful porcelain doll. She wore a deep-green riding skirt and a matching jacket. Her red hair was tucked up in a green riding hat, and there was a fall of lace at her throat.

Margaret looked very pretty too, in a light-yellow dress with tiny white dots all over it and a yellow bonnet. When they reached the cabin, she slid down from the pony and turned to Eliza.

"Would you like to pet my pony?" she asked. "Her name is Apples because apples are her favorite treat."

Caroline and Martha gathered around Eliza, and they each took turns running their hands down Apples' soft nose. But they whirled around when they heard Mother exclaim, "But surely these are not for us?"

Mr. Kellogg was leading the calf forward, and at Mother's feet was the crate. Caroline counted four red hens peering out through the slats.

"You and Mr. Holbrook have been more than helpful to me," Mr. Kellogg said, nodding his head. "I'm happy to be able to wish you well in your new marriage."

Mother looked back and forth between the Kelloggs. Her mouth opened, but she could not speak. Finally she said in a bewildered voice, "But this is much too generous. We cannot possibly accept—"

"Nonsense," Mr. Kellogg interrupted. "You took such good care of my workers last winter. Without you they would have up and left me, I have no doubt. And you took such good care of Addie, I'm happy to have her calf in such able hands." He turned and winked at Caroline. "And I know you'll take good care of the hens, am I right?"

"Yes sir!" Caroline said proudly.

"Margaret already named the calf Baby," Mr. Kellogg continued. "But you may change it if you see fit."

Caroline ran a hand over the calf's soft skin, and the calf raised her head and looked at her with gentle brown eyes.

"Baby is a perfect name," Caroline said, and Margaret grinned.

Mother told Martha to take Baby to the pole barn and then fetch Mr. Holbrook and the boys. Mr. Kellogg carried the crate to the hen-house and left Caroline to make the proper introductions.

Back inside the cabin, Caroline quickly washed her hands and face in the washbasin. Mother had already set the fresh bread and honey on the table. This made Caroline feel a little better. They still had on their old every-day dresses and were dusty from working in the garden, but at least there was Mother's delicious bread to offer their guests.

Mr. Holbrook and the boys arrived and shook hands with Mr. Kellogg. When they were all seated around the table, Mr. Kellogg announced that work would begin on the mill in three weeks' time.

"We have a goodly group of men willing and able to begin digging the mill dam," he said.

Henry pushed the hair out of his eyes. "As

we told you at Camp Meeting, sir, we'll be happy to help," he said.

"Well, we can surely use as many able bodies as there are in these parts," Mr. Kellogg replied.

"The boys are needed here on the farm," Mr. Holbrook said in a firm voice. "We'll not have a chance of clearing this land before the first snowfall unless we keep at it."

"But we told Mr. Kellogg at Camp Meeting we'd help with the mill," Henry cried out.

"Henry," Mother said warningly.

"I'll be happy to dig enough for the three of us," Mr. Holbrook said mildly. "But your place right now is working this land, Henry. I'm sure Mr. Kellogg understands."

"Indeed I do," Mr. Kellogg replied, turning to Henry. "Don't worry, son. There will be more work, rest assured. Concord is growing, and the mill is just the beginning."

Henry nodded politely, but he could not hide the disappointment on his face.

"Will you build a school as well?" Caroline spoke up.

"Do you like to go to school?" Mrs. Kellogg asked Caroline.

"Yes, ma'am. I loved going to school in Brookfield," Caroline answered, feeling suddenly shy under the pretty green gaze.

"Caroline was one of the best spellers for her age," Martha announced.

"One shouldn't boast, Martha, even if it's not for yourself," Mother said quietly.

"Spelling is very important, as I keep reminding my husband." Mrs. Kellogg continued to smile at Caroline, and Mr. Kellogg gave a warm laugh.

"Laura will not rest until Concord has its own school," Mr. Kellogg said. "Now that there are more settlers in these parts, perhaps we'll be able to raise a schoolhouse once the mill is completed."

"If the yellow fever doesn't draw you away first," Mrs. Kellogg said.

"Yellow fever?" Mother asked, her eyes looking worried.

Mr. Kellogg fished a piece of newspaper out

of his vest pocket and spread it out onto the table.

"That's what the papers are calling this mad rush for gold," he explained.

Henry's face lit up again, and he leaned over the table to get a better look. Along the top of the newspaper, headlines ran in bold letters:

INEXHAUSTIBLE GOLD MINES FOUND IN CALIFORNIA!
Tremendous Excitement
Among the Americans!
GREAT RUSH TO THE GOLD REGION!

"Ho for California! That's the cry from here to the Atlantic," Mr. Kellogg said as he passed the paper around. "I myself have caught the bug. I'm sending a team of men to California to prospect for me after the mill is built."

"You mean you're paying men to dig gold for you?" Henry gulped.

"That's right," Mr. Kellogg replied. "There's

a good deal of riches to be earned, by all accounts. But I can't be leaving Laura and Margaret, so I plan to pay any man's way if he's wanting to get to California. I'll also pay a fair wage for all his work once he gets there, so long as he splits his diggings with me."

"Who all is setting to go?" Mr. Holbrook asked.

"Hirch and Burgg. Mason and his boy, too." Caroline recognized the names of the men who had eaten in their kitchen all winter.

"There's a body bringing his son along with him?" Henry asked.

"So long as there's some grown man to look after a boy, I'll send him too," Mr. Kellogg replied. "As a matter of fact, there are a couple of orphan boys who live near you who are going. Hirch has agreed to take charge of them, and they'll be heading out west as well."

"Miles and Wally are going to California?" Caroline cried out. They were two brothers who lived all by themselves in a cabin in the woods. Miles was not very nice, but Wally had always been nice to Caroline. Last winter the boys had been cold and nearly starving; Mother had fed them, and Mr. Holbrook had gone to help them start up their fire again.

Mr. Kellogg nodded.

Henry turned toward Mother and opened his mouth to speak, but Mother's face was stern. "Don't be getting any ideas, Henry Odin Quiner," she said in a voice that meant there would be no arguing.

"I can see there's already a body here with yellow fever." Mr. Kellogg laughed amiably.

"He's got it something awful," Thomas chirped. "He's always talking about gold."

"Foolish notions when there's plenty of riches to be found right here if a body's willing to work for it," Mr. Holbrook said.

Henry's eyes flashed. "I don't see why it's so foolish when it seems like there's just gold out there for the taking. And Mr. Kellogg's paying good money to go look for it."

Mr. Kellogg raised his hand in the air and said in a soothing voice, "Now, young Henry, I know it seems like a sure thing, but one never knows about such ventures. That's why

I'm sending only a small group out first. Come spring, if it proves a success, I'll send another group."

Once more Henry's eyes were bright and glowing, but he did not say anything more. Caroline watched as he fingered the newspaper article. She wondered what he was thinking.

For the rest of the visit they did not speak of gold.

Mr. Kellogg began to discuss the plans for the mill with Joseph and Mr. Holbrook, while Mother and Mrs. Kellogg talked of Boston. They knew many of the same places, because Mrs. Kellogg had also lived there before she was married.

Eliza showed Margaret the loft and the little bedroom with the two plump beds. She brought out the rag doll Mother had made for her last birthday, and Caroline and Martha brought out their dolls as well.

"I wish I lived in a cabin," Margaret said. "It seems very cozy."

Caroline thought of the Kelloggs' grand house on top of Concord Hill, and she knew she would trade places with Margaret in a second if she could. But then she immediately felt guilty for having such naughty thoughts. Mother had made the cabin their home, and it was true that there was a wonderful close feeling when they were all together under its little roof.

At last the Kelloggs announced they must be going.

"We won't keep you from your work any longer," Mr. Kellogg said as they walked into the yard. Mrs. Kellogg took Mother's hand and thanked her for the wonderful refreshment.

"Small thanks for the kindness you have shown us," Mother said gratefully.

Later that evening, long after the Kelloggs were gone, Henry went to the pole barn with Caroline to check on Baby.

"Mr. Kellogg sure is a wealthy man if he can pay other folks to dig gold for him," Henry said, taking something out of his trouser pocket. Caroline saw that it was the newspaper article Mr. Kellogg had brought. "He gave it to me to keep," Henry explained. "It says here that the gold is just running down the mountains in rivers out there."

Caroline looked over her brother's arm, squinting at the small print in the dim light. Henry sighed as he carefully folded the paper up again and tucked it back into his pocket.

"I don't care what old Holbrook says," Henry mumbled. "There's no riches here, only more hard work. I'm bound to get to California one way or another."

"But Henry, you're only thirteen years old!" Caroline cried. "Why would you want to leave us and go tearing off to the other side of the country?"

"Wouldn't you like pretty dresses and to ride a pony like Margaret?" Henry asked. His face was flushed, and his eyes were faraway-looking. Suddenly Caroline knew why they called it yellow fever. Henry looked almost sick with wanting.

"I would like pretty dresses and a pony." Caroline spoke slowly, thinking carefully as she said the words. "But I'd much rather have you here safe and sound with us."

Henry's face cleared, and he reached out and tugged on Caroline's braid. "Don't worry about me, Little Brownbraid," he said, grinning his old donkey grin.

It felt so good to see Henry smiling again, Caroline didn't want to scold him for calling her the old nickname. Together they fed Baby some grain and spoke to her and stroked her soft hide so she wouldn't miss Addie and her old home too much.

"This is your home now, and don't forget it," Caroline said softly, and she realized she wasn't speaking only to the new calf, but to Henry as well.

The Mill Dam

"The men from town are beginning to dig the mill dam today," Mother announced one morning as she spooned warm mush into the bowls. "Frederick has gone to help with the digging. He'll not return till after supper."

"Did the boys go too?" Eliza asked.

Mother shook her head. "The boys are needed here. They're clearing more land."

After the breakfast dishes had been washed and put away, Caroline saw to the geese and hens. Henry had already let Baby out of the pole barn. Caroline could hear the bell they had tied around her neck ringing softly through the trees. All day long Baby roamed around the little woods, grazing on sweet grasses. At evening time Caroline and Eliza would listen for the bell and go find her and lead her home.

After bringing the morning's eggs into the cabin, Caroline joined Mother and Martha and Eliza, who were in the garden picking the summer vegetables. Caroline thought summer was the best time of all, because there were fresh peppers and peas and beans and tomatoes and melons. And there was always fish from the river or a plump jackrabbit Joseph or Henry or Mr. Holbrook brought back at the end of the day.

"I remember the mill in Brookfield," Eliza said thoughtfully as she walked along the rows behind Mother carrying a vegetable basket. "It was made of wood and stone."

"That is correct." Mother nodded in her calico bonnet.

"Then why are the men digging the mill

here in Concord?" Eliza asked.

"Well, you'll be able to see for yourself," Mother said, straightening up and placing a handful of beans in the basket. "We'll fix a dinner for Frederick, and you girls can carry it to him."

"All the way to Concord?" Caroline asked excitedly.

Mother nodded and smiled. "Now, quickly girls, let's finish up here. You'll need time enough to make the journey to Concord."

Going down the garden rows became a race. Even Martha joined in. Each tried to see who could pick the fastest and have the most in her basket. Caroline reached the end of her row first. Her basket was overflowing with peas and peppers. Martha was next with a basket full of tomatoes.

"No fair," Eliza whined, holding out her basket only half filled with yellow squash.

But Mother was cheerful. "No frowns. We must be thankful for such a wealthy harvest," she said as they walked back toward the cabin. Caroline noticed that since she had married

Mr. Holbrook, Mother did not seem to worry so much anymore.

Martha stirred the rabbit stew that had been simmering on the cookstove all morning while Caroline wrapped a fresh warm loaf of bread in a piece of linen. Eliza helped Mother make ginger water, a special treat for such a hot day.

"You may wait while Frederick eats his dinner," Mother instructed. "There's enough for him to share it with others. Then hurry back with the basket and tins. I'll keep your own dinner warm for you until you return."

When everything was ready, Mother made certain the girls' faces and hands were scrubbed and their braids were neat. Then she handed the pot of stew to Martha. Caroline carried the jar of ginger water with a clean cloth tied over the top. Eliza carried the basket with the bread and the tin plates, spoons, and cups.

"How will we know where the men are digging?" Martha asked.

"Follow the road into Concord and then keep going straight at the crossroads. You'll run into the river, and you'll find the men there," Mother said. "Now, I expect you to come straight back as soon as Frederick has eaten. No time for dawdling in the woods."

"Yes, ma'am," the girls answered all together.

"Come along, Wolf!" Caroline called, and the dog bounded up, barking happily and leading them down the leafy green path toward the Territorial Road.

"We're going on an adventure!" Eliza cried.

The girls chattered merrily as they wound their way through the dense growth of trees, watching for roots and stones that might trip them and make them spill their precious cargo. The air was still, and mosquitoes buzzed in swarms in the marshy places. Sometimes the droning sound of the cicadas' humming drowned out everything.

When they reached the Territorial Road, they rested their arms for a little while, setting their things down carefully. The sky was hazy and there were still no cooling breezes. A covered wagon passed slowly by, with the words "California or bust" written in black lettering along the side. Caroline thought of Henry and was glad he was not there to see. He might try jump onto the wagon and stow away. A little girl with long blond braids and a blue bonnet waved from the back.

At the crossroads they continued straight as Mother had instructed. They all looked up as they passed the Kelloggs' fine house on the hill. Its many windowpanes glinted in the sun.

"I wonder if Margaret is outside playing," Eliza said, but they did not see anyone on the great lawn.

They came through another little stretch of woods, and soon they could hear loud voices. Caroline saw a group of men up ahead through the trees. They were leaning on their shovels and axes near the water.

"Anybody seed Joe Springer of late?" a man asked, and another man spoke up.

"I heard he took his wife and son and headed west to hunt for gold."

"He took off all right, but it weren't on

account of the gold," an elderly man with a long white beard said. "I heard tell he took off on account of the fever."

"Yellow fever, you mean," a man said.

"No sirree." White beard paused and spat a stream of tobacco juice on the ground. "I'm talking about the fever that's killing folk in Milwaukee."

Caroline and Martha and Eliza stopped cold and looked from one to the other, wondering if they had heard right.

"Who says folk are dying in Milwaukee?" a voice asked.

"I'm a-saying it," white beard announced, and the other men moved closer. "My cousin owns a tavern in Milwaukee, and he sent word about a man who was seen strolling down the street healthy as an ox one day and lying cold as stone the next. Word's spreading. Cholera."

There was a hush in the woods as the men went quiet. Suddenly Wolf burst out from under some brush next to Caroline. All the men turned and looked.

"What a pretty bunch of posies to be sneaking around in these here woods," white beard said.

Caroline felt her face grow hot. "We weren't sneaking around," she answered stoutly. "We're bringing dinner for Mr. Holbrook."

The men guffawed, and one of them pointed toward the right.

"Holbrook's downriver a piece, with the other crew. But you can leave those fixin's with me, and I'll be happy to see he gets 'em."

Martha stepped forward. "Thank you, sir, but our mother told us to make sure and give the food to our pa."

There was another round of laughter. The elderly man said, "You're good girls, I can see. Well then, follow the river, and you can't miss 'im."

"Thank you, sir," Martha said politely, and turned in the direction they had pointed.

"Come along, Wolf," Caroline called. She and Eliza quickly followed behind.

"We must hurry home and tell Mother about

the fever," Caroline said urgently as they walked. "What if that man they were talking about was Uncle Elisha?"

"Nonsense," Martha said stoutly. "Milwaukee is a big city. Grandma would have sent word. And who knows if those men are even speaking the truth. They seemed like rough characters to me."

Caroline took comfort from Martha's words, but the happiness of the morning was disturbed, and the girls fell silent. They followed the bend in the river until they heard many deep voices singing all together.

"Oh, do you remember Sweet Betsy
  from Pike,
Who crossed the wide prairie with her
  lover Ike
With two yoke of oxen, a big yeller dog,
A tall Shanghai rooster, and one spotted hog?

Hoodle dang fol-de-di-do,
Hoodle dang fol-de-day."

Caroline felt like giggling at the silly words she had never heard before. When she came out from among the trees, she saw that there were about twenty men working in a line along the bank of the river. Their shovels sank into the soft soil and then flashed upward, sending chunks of earth into a great mound of dirt in the river. The mound was taller than Caroline.

Mr. Holbrook was in the middle of the line. He did not sing with the others, but he worked steadily. When he paused to wipe his brow, he caught sight of the girls and waved a hand in the air. He continued to dig for a little while longer; then a great call went out, and he and the other men stopped, pushing their shovels upright into the ground and sloshing through the mud.

The girls approached. "Mother asked us to bring your dinner." Martha held out the stew for Mr. Holbrook to see. "She said there is enough for you to share."

"Well, I'm much obliged," Mr. Holbrook said, and beckoned to a few of the men nearby.

They all walked up a little hill to where the grass was soft and clean. Caroline and Martha and Eliza sat on the grass in the shade and watched as Mr. Holbrook divided out the food. The other men moved off a little to sit on the big boulders under the pine trees, and Mr. Holbrook joined the girls.

There were men on the far side of the river as well, and they were all sitting and eating from baskets or dinner pails. Some leaned against trees and pulled out their pipes. The men laughed and joked quietly as they ate or smoked. Caroline thought it was a nice feeling to be sitting along the river with so many neighbors.

After a while Eliza leaned forward a little. "Pa?" she asked in a tentative voice.

"Yes, Eliza?"

"Why are you digging up the river? I asked Mother, but she said I would see for myself when I got here. But I don't see."

"Well now," Mr. Holbrook said. "We're aiming to build a dam to stop up part of the river."

"But why?" Eliza asked.

The Mill Dam

Mr. Holbrook took a bite of bread and drink of ginger water before answering. "A mill needs a waterwheel to do all its milling," he explained. "And the waterwheel needs a force of water flowing beneath it day and night, pushing it around and around. The river in these parts doesn't flow fast enough in any one place to keep the wheel turning. So first we have to build a dam out of dirt and logs to create a rush of water. We're piling the dirt up now; then we'll lay logs over it. The dam will force the river into a smaller channel, so the water will move quicker."

Caroline remembered going to the mill in Brookfield with Mother and watching the huge waterwheel that groaned and churned and spat foamy water off its paddles high into the air. Inside the mill there was always dust everywhere that tickled her nose, and there were broken wheat kernels that crunched beneath her feet.

"How long will it take you to finish the mill?" Caroline asked.

"Well, first we have to dam up the river,"

Mr. Holbrook answered. "Then we'll have to haul enough logs and split them into planks to raise the mill."

"The mill in Brookfield was big," Eliza said.

"It was three stories high," Caroline added.

"That's about right," Mr. Holbrook said. "I reckon our mill will be three stories high as well. They need all those rooms to hold the grain before it goes to the grindstone, and then they need enough room to hold all the flour and cornmeal after it's been ground and sacked."

"It sounds like it will take forever to build the mill," Eliza said.

"I reckon not," Mr. Holbrook replied. "We've got a good crew, so I'm hoping it won't keep me from clearing our own land too long."

Caroline thought of her brothers working all by themselves on the land. She hoped Mr. Holbrook was right.

Soon the men along the river began to stretch their legs and walk back toward the water. The girls packed up the spoons and plates and cups, and Mr. Holbrook thanked them for bringing the fixings.

"Put your shoulder into it, men," someone called, and the work began again. Shovels flashed and dirt flew. A deep voice began to sing a new song:

"Farewell to old England the beautiful!
Farewell to my old pals as well!
Farewell to the famous Old Bailey
Where I used to cut such a swell.

"My too-ral li roo-lal li laity
Too-ral li roo-lal li lay
Too-ral li roo-lal li laity
Too-ral li roo-lal li lay!"

Caroline followed Martha and Eliza back through the woods, the singing getting farther and farther away. As they were passing the first group of men, Caroline let out a little gasp. Henry was standing with his ax over his shoulder, talking with the elderly man with the long white beard.

Martha had seen Henry too. "Henry Odin Quiner!" she called loudly, mimicking Mother's scolding voice.

Henry looked around, startled. But when he saw it was Martha, not Mother, he did not look ashamed at all. He grinned his donkey grin as he strode up the hill to the girls. "I've done all the clearing I can stand to do in one day on Holbrook's place," he said. "Figured I'd come down and help out like I told Mr. Kellogg I would."

"But Mr. Holbrook—Pa—he's just down at the bend in the river, he'll surely see you—" Caroline began.

"And he's sure to tan your hide for disobeying him," Martha finished.

"Nohow," Henry scoffed. "I'll stay clear of him, don't you worry. There's plenty of work crews, so he'll be none the wiser. Unless . . ." Henry squinted at his sisters. "Unless one of you gets a notion to tell on me."

Caroline reluctantly shook her head. She did not think what Henry was doing was right, but she would never tattle.

"I won't tell," Eliza said, following Caroline's lead.

"I'll not tell unless you give me reason to," said Martha.

"But what about Joseph and Thomas?" Caroline asked, glancing around. "Are they here too?"

Henry gave a quick shake of his head. "Joseph was none too happy I left, but he said he'd do the extra work for me, so Holbrook can't say we're shirking."

Caroline felt sorry for Joseph. With Mr. Holbrook and Henry both gone, he was doing the work of three. She thought it was selfish of Henry to run off and leave him. It seemed there were plenty of men to dig the mill dam.

"Any of that left for me?" Henry asked, peeking into the basket.

There was one piece of bread, and Eliza handed it to Henry. He grinned and then strode back down the hill to the men.

"See you at supper," he called out over his shoulder.

The girls did not speak as they walked home along the Territorial Road. They passed more wagons with folks peering out the front and back. None had writing on them, but Caroline wondered if they were all headed for California too. Suddenly she remembered what the men had said about folks fleeing because of sickness.

"We forgot to ask Pa about the fever!" Caroline cried.

"We can ask him when he gets home tonight," Martha said matter-of-factly. "I'm sure those men were just gabbing. I told you before, we would have gotten a letter from Grandma if something terrible had happened."

Caroline was not so sure, but she kept quiet until they were back at the cottage.

"The men down at the mill were talking about a fever!" she cried as soon as she saw Mother.

"Goodness!" Mother raised her eyebrows, setting down the pan of stew she was holding. "What's all this about?"

"We overheard some men talking about a

terrible fever." Caroline spoke more slowly.

"You mean the yellow fever," Mother said, and she went back to dishing the stew into tin bowls for the girls. "Don't you remember that's what Mr. Kellogg called this foolishness over gold?"

Caroline shook her head fiercely. "No, ma'am. It was a different kind of fever. A real fever. This man said folks were dying in Milwaukee."

Mother held up her hand for silence. She had the girls wash up and sit down nicely at the table. Then she turned to Martha and asked, "Is this true, what Caroline is saying?"

Martha shrugged. "We heard one man tell of how a fellow had died in Milwaukee." She dipped a spoon into her beans. "It frightened Caroline and Eliza is all."

Caroline knew it had frightened Martha, too, but she did not say so. Mother never liked to hear the girls bickering among themselves.

"What did Frederick have to say about this talk?" Mother asked.

"We forgot to ask him because we were

watching the digging," Eliza said.

Mother smiled. "You see now why the men are digging up the river?"

"Yes, ma'am," Eliza answered. "I like digging in the garden, but I'm glad I don't have to dig up a whole river."

Mother let out a little laugh. Then she reached out and patted Caroline on the shoulder. "Don't worry," she said. "I'll speak with Frederick tonight. I'm sure there is nothing to worry about."

The girls spent the rest of the day helping Mother begin the pickling and preserving of the garden vegetables. Caroline forgot all about Henry until late in the day, when she and Eliza were leading Baby back from the riverbank. Henry snuck up behind them and gave his hoot-owl cry.

"You can't scare me!" Caroline said, and Henry tugged on her braid.

"I told you the old man wouldn't catch on." Henry grinned. His face was dirty, and his shirt was streaked with mud.

"I don't think what you're doing is right,"

Caroline said firmly.

"Me neither," Eliza chimed in.

"Well, I don't think it's right for Holbrook to tell me I can't do something I already promised to do," Henry said stubbornly.

"Mr. Holbrook is your pa now," Caroline said. "You should do what he says."

Henry pushed the hair out of his eyes and scowled. "He's not my pa," he mumbled.

Caroline felt her insides tighten into a knot. She was about to say something back, but they were nearing the cabin and Mother was outside speaking with Mr. Holbrook. Her face looked worried.

At supper neither Mother nor Mr. Holbrook spoke about the fever, and Caroline did not like to ask. But later, after the girls had changed into their nightgowns, Mother came and sat on the edge of their bed.

"It seems that the men on the riverbank were speaking the truth," Mother said in her quiet voice. Caroline and Martha exchanged glances. "But I do not want you to worry. It seems there have been only a few cases of fever. I'm sure all is well at Uncle Elisha's house." Mother leaned forward and kissed each of them on the forehead. "Now say your prayers like good girls and go to sleep."

Caroline knelt on the hardwood floor beside her sisters. Silently she said an extra prayer for Grandma and Uncle Elisha and Aunt Margaret and the cousins.

Each morning over the next few weeks Mr. Holbrook went off to dig the mill dam in the gray light of dawn. Caroline and her sisters did not go to the river every day. Sometimes Mr. Holbrook took his own dinner or shared food with the other workers. When the girls did go, it was exciting to see how the river was changing. It was getting narrower and narrower as the men created a great wall of dirt and logs. Other men worked to clear the trees and brush along the opposite bank.

At dinnertime Caroline liked sitting with the men and listening to them joke and sing. Although there was much talk of gold, she never heard anyone mention cholera again, and she tried to put her worries out of her mind.

Sometimes on their way home they caught sight of Henry. He would wave and smile, but Caroline always turned her head away. She felt torn inside. She would never tell on Henry, but just like knowing about Mr. Holbrook's proposal months ago, keeping the secret of Henry's naughtiness began to feel like a weight pressing against her chest.

One day near the end of August the girls arrived at the river and the dam was nearly finished. Huge logs had been laid over the top of the dam of dirt and smaller logs, completely stopping the flow of water except in one place. There the water rushed forward into a large pond where there had been only trees and brush before.

"That pond will be full of fish and wild ducks in no time," Mr. Holbrook explained as he ate his dinner. "And in the winter folks can go ice-skating."

"Ice-skating!" Eliza cried.

"Back in Connecticut when I was a boy, we used to ice-skate on the millpond," Mr. Holbrook said. "I used to go racing up and

163

down as fast as the wind."

Caroline looked up at Mr. Holbrook's sharp features. He did everything with a great deal of care and thought. It was hard to imagine him racing as fast as the wind. It was hard to imagine him as a boy, too.

"We don't have any ice skates," Eliza said sadly.

Mr. Holbrook thought for a moment, and then he said, "Who knows what Santeclaus will bring at Christmastime."

Caroline smiled to see Eliza's face light up so. In the hot August weather Christmas seemed far away.

Now that the dam was finished, work on the mill itself began. The girls no longer carried dinner to Mr. Holbrook. Mother said the woods were too dangerous now for little girls to go walking about. The work crews were busy chopping down enough tall trees to raise the mill.

Caroline knew that Henry was still running off to help the men after dinner. Sometimes she came upon Joseph in the woods. He waved and smiled but rarely stopped to talk because he was so busy. Joseph had grown taller over the summer months. His muscles were strong from all the work, and the lines of his face were more defined. Caroline was surprised to notice one day that he looked more like a man now than a boy. Even little Thomas looked older as he dragged kindling and brush to the bonfires and helped Joseph turn up the soil, which was full of roots and rocks.

Caroline did not speak about Henry to her brothers, but she hoped that the mill would be finished soon so she would not have to feel deceitful all the time.

Finally, one day, all the lies came tumbling out into the open. Mr. Holbrook arrived home early from working on the mill. When Caroline caught sight of him walking through the woods with Joseph and Thomas and no Henry, her heart began to beat very fast. She and Eliza looked at each other but did not say a word. They drove Baby to the pole barn and fed her and hurried to the cabin.

Inside, Mother's face was set in a hard

frown. She told Caroline and Eliza to wash up and set the table, as there would be an early supper. Joseph and Thomas were already seated. Thomas had his chin against his chest, sniffling a little.

No one spoke a word during supper. Caroline hardly tasted a bite of Mother's rabbit stew. She kept listening for Henry. Her breath caught in her throat when she heard him whistling as he walked between the trees. When he reached the open cabin door, he stopped cold.

"I was just—" Henry began, but Mr. Holbrook's deep voice cut him off.

"I wouldn't bother digging yourself any deeper, if I were you, son. Joseph has already owned up to everything."

Henry's cheeks flamed a bright red. He looked down at his dirt-streaked hands, not knowing what to do. Mr. Holbrook's face was stern, and Mother's eyes flashed angrily. Her voice was sharp when she spoke. "Wash up and sit down, Henry."

Henry hurried to do as he was told. When

he was seated, he looked at his plate without raising a fork.

"I am ashamed to think, Henry Odin Quiner," Mother began, "how you've been deceiving us all this time." Mother turned to Joseph. "And I'm ashamed of you, as well, Joseph. You are the oldest, and you should have known better. Keeping your brother's secret is just the same as lying."

Joseph's brown eyes were more pained than Caroline had ever seen them. Thomas had tears streaming down his cheeks, and Eliza had begun to cry as well. Caroline's eyes stung, but she did not cry. She felt as if she could hardly breathe. She knew she had kept Henry's secret, so she had been lying too.

"Now, Charlotte." Mr. Holbrook's voice finally broke the terrible silence. He did not sound as angry as Mother, and Caroline looked at his face in surprise. His jaw was set firmly and he was not smiling, but his eyes did not flash fiercely like Mother's. "The boys are spirited, but I reckon they're not all bad, are you, sons?"

All three shook their heads and waited for Mr. Holbrook to continue.

"Joseph did a mountain of work trying to labor for two, and Thomas was a mighty help as far as I can tell." Mr. Holbrook paused. Then he cleared his throat, and his blue eyes focused on Henry. "I will say this only once. 'If a house be divided against itself, that house cannot stand.'" Mr. Holbrook took a sip of coffee and pushed his plate away. Caroline knew she had heard those words before, but she wasn't sure where.

"Now, Henry, I expect you back to work clearing the land tomorrow," Mr. Holbrook continued. "All day. The mill will be raised in a matter of days, I'm reckoning. So God willing, I'll be back to help by week's end."

"Yes sir," Joseph spoke up. They all waited breathlessly for Henry's barely audible "Yes sir."

Mr. Holbrook gave a nod and stood up. "Now if you'll excuse me, I'd like to take a walk along the fields to see how the corn is growing." He put on his hat and left the room.

No one said a word. Caroline made her-self finish the stew even though she was not hungry. She could not believe that Mr. Holbrook had not punished Henry. Henry looked stunned as well. As soon as supper was over, he jumped up to fill the wood box. He carried the biggest logs and merely shook his head when Joseph and Thomas offered to help.

There was no singing or checkers playing that night. Mother said they were all to go to bed early. As she laid her head against her pil-low and closed her eyes, Caroline could smell Mr. Holbrook's tobacco, but the house was terribly still.

For the rest of that week, it seemed every-one was walking around on tiptoes. Henry went off with Joseph and Thomas in the morn-ing. He did not smile or tease, but he did not complain either. Caroline went about her chores with a heavy heart. Everything had been going so well with Mr. Holbrook as their new pa. Now Henry had ruined it, and things were not right in the little house.

On Friday Mr. Holbrook came home at suppertime and announced that the mill was finished.

"I reckon we should take a gander over to Concord tomorrow so's you can all see the mill with your own eyes," he said.

Thomas clapped his hands together, and Caroline felt her heart lightening a little.

The next day, after the morning chores were done, they all set out. It was just like when they had gone to Camp Meeting at the start of summer, but Caroline was glad there would be no Reverend Speakes at the end of the trail.

After the crossroads Eliza took Thomas's hand and led him through the patch of woods. "This is the way," she said.

The mill stood tall and majestic on the opposite bank. It was three stories high, with sturdy walls made of newly split oak planks and a slanting roof made from hand-cut shingles. There were a few large glass windows gleaming in the sunlight. The waterwheel churned busily at the side, and a little bridge ran from a doorway above the waterwheel over the dam to the near side of the pond. The pond itself was a large, still body of water. Already there were wild ducks floating here and there over the clear water.

There were other folks strolling along the banks, admiring the new mill. Caroline recognized many of the men she had seen digging the dam. They held their heads up proudly as they walked with their wives and children. Standing with Mr. Holbrook gazing at the mill, Caroline felt a sense of pride as well. She realized it was the same feeling she had known in Brookfield when she had looked at the church and the other places Father had helped to build.

"A job well done," Caroline heard a familiar voice say, and she turned to see Mr. Kellogg coming through the small crowd, greeting each man with a firm handshake and each lady with a tip of his hat. His wife was not there, but Margaret was skipping along beside him. When he reached them, Mr. Kellogg bowed to Mother and slapped Mr. Holbrook on the back.

"Good work, Holbrook," he said. "I declare this to be the finest mill in Wisconsin."

Mr. Holbrook gave his quick nod. "Henry put in some time as well," he said without turning to look at Henry.

Mr. Kellogg reached out and shook Henry's hand. "Well, then, young man, you did a good job," he said.

"Thank you, sir," Henry replied, but he looked at Mr. Holbrook when he said it.

Mr. Kellogg took a turn with them along the bank. The day was warm, but there was a pleasant breeze coming off the water. Caroline liked the way the whole sky, with its patches of white wispy clouds, seemed to be reflected in the pretty pond.

"Pa says we can ice-skate here in winter," Eliza told Margaret.

"I've never been ice-skating, have you?" Margaret asked, and Eliza shook her head.

"I used to go ice-skating on the millpond in Boston with my brothers when I was a girl," Mother said wistfully. Her face looked so pretty and serene under her bonnet, Caroline almost let out a little sigh. Everything had been so tense around the house since Henry's scolding. Now the world seemed right once more. Caroline hoped with all her heart that their house would never be divided again.

Trip to Watertown

August turned into September, and yet the days continued to burn hot and still. The nights were marked by sudden flashes of lightning and bursts of thunder. But the heat and quick rainstorms were never enough to do any real damage, and so the corn grew tall in the field and the crops that had been planted late in the season were thriving.

For several days Mr. Holbrook and the boys stopped clearing trees and went to the marshy places along the river where the wild hay grew.

They cut the long golden grasses with sharp scythes and then tied them into great bundles. Now Baby would have plenty to keep her warm and fed during the fall and winter.

One afternoon at dinner, Mr. Holbrook turned to Caroline and asked, "Well, do you think those geese of yours are fat enough to fetch a fair price at the market?"

Caroline sat a little taller in her seat. Mr. Holbrook was asking her opinion as if she were an adult, and it made Caroline feel very important.

"Yes, sir," she answered solemnly. "All the geese are nice and plump."

"Well, then," Mr. Holbrook said, "it's time to make the trip to the Watertown market."

"When will you leave?" Mother asked.

"Day after tomorrow," Mr. Holbrook answered, considering.

"But how will you get the geese all the way to Watertown?" Caroline asked. She knew Watertown was a long way off, so far that none of the Quiners had been there yet. She imagined Mr. Holbrook driving the gaggle of silly

175

birds down the road with a stick, and the thought almost made her laugh.

"I've traded work with Mr. Kellogg for the loan of his wagon and team of oxen," Mr. Holbrook answered. "It's a good two-day journey there and two days back. I reckon Joseph should stay here and mind things while I'm away, being the oldest, but I'd like Henry to come with me. " He turned to Henry. "That is, if you're willing."

Henry's head shot up in surprise. His mouth was full of corn bread, and he had to work to swallow before he answered loudly, "Yes, sir!"

And so all that day and the next, Mr. Holbrook was busy making wooden crates for the geese. Joseph and Henry helped split the logs into small slats while Thomas helped hammer the slats together.

Mother and the girls were busy too. The geese were not the only things Mr. Holbrook would take with him to trade at the market. There was ash from the ash pile to pack into cloth sacks, and there were the hens' eggs. All summer long they had taken what they needed and packed the rest of the eggs carefully in a barrel of sawdust. Now Mr. Holbrook would take the barrel to Watertown.

Once the ash and eggs were ready, Mother set about preparing enough food for the journey. The girls helped make beans and johnnycake.

Finally Mr. Holbrook sent Joseph to fetch the wagon from Mr. Kellogg. Now that so many trees had been cleared, there was a little wagon path that ran along the side of the garden. When Caroline heard the jingle of the reins and the creak of wagon wheels, she and Eliza came running from inside the cabin. They patted Mr. Kellogg's oxen along their stiff brown coats.

Bright and early the next morning, everyone was up and out of bed before the first rooster crowed. Caroline helped guide all but four of the geese into their crates. Mr. Holbrook said they would hold back these four so there would be another flock next year. The goslings were as big as their parents now. They waddled and honked and snapped, but soon they were all inside.

"Will you miss your geese?" Eliza asked, and Caroline shook her head. She still liked the clucking hens better.

Henry and Joseph secured the crates to the wagon bed with long leather straps. "Don't you wish you could come too?" Henry asked Caroline.

"I wish I could see the market," Caroline admitted. "But I'm glad I don't have to sit in a bumpy old wagon for two days."

"I could ride this wagon clear across to the Pacific Ocean!" Henry's eyes were bright, and he had a faraway smile across his face. Caroline had not heard her brother speak of the gold rush in many weeks, but she realized that he still had dreams of going to California. It gave her a worried feeling.

When all had been packed securely, Mr. Holbrook stepped up to the wagon seat and took the reins. Henry gave Caroline a wink and jumped up beside him.

"A safe journey," Mother called.

Mr. Holbrook's eyes crinkled as he looked down at her kindly. "Don't worry, Charlotte," he said in a soft voice Caroline had not heard before. "We'll be back as soon as we're able."

"Watertown or bust!" Henry yelled, waving his hat in the air and sending Eliza and Thomas into a fit of giggles.

"Giddap," Mr. Holbrook called, and the oxen plodded forward. Wolf barked at the wheels, and Thomas and Eliza ran behind the wagon as far as the end of the cornfield, then turned and raced back. Henry gave one last wave of his hat before the wagon rounded the bend and was lost from sight.

That night the cabin seemed very empty without Henry and Mr. Holbrook. Though Mr. Holbrook had been living with them only a short time, Caroline missed his strong, quiet presence. Mother rocked in her rocker, mending and humming, and the girls sewed on their quilts. Joseph tried to play checkers with Thomas, but Thomas was more interested in playing with the wooden horses and the two little wooden men Mr. Holbrook had whittled for him.

"Will Pa and Henry come straight back after the market?" Thomas asked.

"No," Mother answered, not looking up from her needle. "They will spend one night in Watertown, and then start along home at first light."

The days passed slowly. Now that the summer vegetables had been harvested, there was more time. In the afternoons the girls studied their lessons. They had been too busy all summer long to study anything but Bible verses on Sundays. As Caroline turned the pages of her worn yellow primer, she thought about Mr. and Mrs. Kellogg and hoped there would be a schoolhouse soon.

On the fourth night Mr. Holbrook and Henry had been gone, Caroline was nearly dozing over her sewing when the snort of oxen and the creaking of wagon wheels jolted her awake.

"It's Pa and Henry!" Thomas cried, rushing to the door.

"It can't be," Mother said uncertainly. "They won't be back until tomorrow."

They all hurried into the yard, and sure enough, there sat the wagon in the bright moonlight, with Mr. Holbrook and Henry staring down at them.

"Why, Frederick! Henry!" Mother exclaimed. "We did not expect you back so soon."

"We couldn't stay in Watertown any longer, on account of—"

Mr. Holbrook put a hand over Henry's arm, and Henry immediately stopped speaking.

"We did a good day's trading yesterday," Mr. Holbrook said. "There was no need to stay any longer."

Henry opened his mouth to say something else, but once again Mr. Holbrook seemed to stop him. Caroline moved closer. Henry's face was pale, and his eyes looked tired. Mr.

Holbrook also looked weary. The lines along his face seemed deeper, and his eyes were red rimmed.

"You must have driven all night and day," Mother said with concern. "Hurry inside. I'll have something warmed up for you in no time."

Joseph helped unload the wagon, and then he led the oxen away to the pole barn so they could eat and rest beside Baby for the night. Caroline and Eliza and Thomas stood staring at the barrels and packages wrapped in brown paper that had come all the way from Watertown. Caroline wanted to know right away what was inside, but she knew Mr. Holbrook would want to eat first.

As soon as Mother had heated up the supper, everyone gathered around while Mr. Holbrook and Henry sat at the table. They ate heartily, and then Mr. Holbrook sighed and said in a weary voice, "It's good to be home."

"We're glad you're back safe and sound," Mother murmured. She smiled at Mr. Holbrook with her eyes.

He nodded and said, "Caroline's geese fetched a good price. I was able to get a wagon-load of stores. There's a barrel of salt pork and a sack each of cornmeal, flour, and salt. Nutmeg, brown sugar, and a little white as well. And a tin of coffee."

Mother's face glowed in the candlelight. Caroline could tell she was happy that there would be plenty in the pantry come winter. They all watched expectantly as Mr. Holbrook stood up and pulled out two packages wrapped in brown paper. "These are for you and the girls," he said, handing them to Mother.

Mother opened the packages, and Caroline saw that there were two large pieces of good strong woollen cloth, one piece of rich brown and one of dark blue. The girls reached out to gently touch the soft fabric. The material wasn't fancy, but it meant there would be new everyday dresses. There was also white cloth for new aprons, instead of the much-mended ones they had worn through the summer.

"What do you say, girls?" Mother prompted.

"Oh, thank you, Pa," Caroline said breathlessly, and Martha and Eliza said their thank-yous too.

"And lookee here," Henry said, pulling a jackknife from his trouser pocket and holding it out for everyone to see. "There's one for Joseph and Thomas too!"

Mr. Holbrook reached into his own pocket and pulled out two more jackknives. He handed the bigger one to Joseph. "Thought it was about time the boys had their own knives to whittle with," he said simply.

Joseph's eyes were nearly as bright as Thomas' as he ran his finger carefully over the silver blade. "Thank you, sir," he said.

Thomas rushed up and wrapped his arms around Mr. Holbrook's legs, almost knocking him over. Mr. Holbrook chuckled and patted Thomas on the back. "You're mighty welcome."

Mr. Holbrook had also brought back a new almanac and a *Godey's Lady's Book*. "I know how you like to keep up with the goings on back east," he said as he handed the magazine to Mother. Caroline could hardly wait to look through the pages.

After the stores had been put away in the pantry and root cellar, Caroline followed Henry to the pole barn to make sure the oxen were secure on their picket lines. Mr. Holbrook said they would take them back to Mr. Kellogg first thing in the morning.

"What was Watertown like?" Caroline asked. She wondered if it was like Brookfield. "Is it—"

"It was terrible," Henry said harshly, startling her. He glanced quickly around to make sure no one was listening. Then he looked at Caroline with an expression that frightened her. "Folks were dying, Caroline. Houses were all boarded up, and everybody was scared."

Caroline felt herself begin to shiver a little despite the warm night air. She hugged her arms around her body. "Pa didn't say anything about that," she whispered. "Are you making this up to scare me, Henry?"

"I couldn't make it up," Henry said, shaking his head fiercely.

"But how did you do your trading?" Caroline asked.

"Folks came from all over to go to the market because no one knew," Henry explained. "But when they saw how bad things were, they did their business fast as they could and hightailed out of there, same as us. I don't know what the fever is, but folks say it's mighty powerful."

"Cholera," Caroline whispered. "That's what the men at the mill were talking about this summer."

Henry grabbed Caroline's arm. "Don't say nothing about what I've told you. Pa doesn't want to scare you all."

Silently Caroline nodded. Baby looked at them with large brown eyes from inside the lean-to, and the oxen snorted loudly through their big nostrils. Caroline realized she should be happy that Henry was at last calling Mr. Holbrook Pa, but as she watched Henry secure the lines that held the oxen, she could think of nothing but the terrible fever.

Back inside the cabin Mr. Holbrook was

sitting by the hearth, showing Thomas, beside him, how to care for the new knife. Mother was sitting in her rocker again, but her face was not serene as it usually was when she sewed. There were lines across her forehead, and Caroline knew that Mr. Holbrook had told her about the cholera. They both looked white and drawn.

That night, Caroline awoke with a start to a rustling beside her. The room was still dark, but she realized Mother was stirring on the other side of the quilt wall.

"Is it morning?" Caroline asked.

"No, Caroline, go back to sleep," Mother's firm voice said, so Caroline rolled over and slept. When she woke again, there was a little light coming through the window and there was a strange sound in the room. As she sat up, she realized it was the sound of heavy, labored breathing. She got up and peered around the edge of the quilt. Mr. Holbrook was lying there with the covers pulled up around him as if he were still asleep, but his eyes were open and staring at the ceiling. His face was terribly white, and there were beads of water on his forehead. Caroline let out a little cry, but Mr. Holbrook did not seem to hear. Mother came quickly into the room.

"It's all right," she said, but Caroline could see the worry in her eyes. "Wake your sisters and come quickly. Bring your clothes. You'll change in the big room this morning."

Martha was already sitting up, looking fearfully toward the quilt wall. "I'll get the clothing, Caroline. You take Eliza," she ordered, and for once Caroline didn't mind her grown-up tone. Quickly the girls left the room.

"What's wrong with Pa?" Eliza asked sleepily as Caroline dressed her.

"He has a bit of fever, that's all," Mother said, but her voice was unsteady. "I want you to hurry and wash up, and then I want you to help Joseph and Thomas carry water from the river. We'll need extra water today."

"What about Henry?" Caroline asked, looking quickly toward the loft.

"Henry is sick as well," Mother said in a quiet voice.

Caroline's heart began to pound, and she felt like bursting into tears, but she knew she had to be strong and help Mother. She washed her hands and face and braided her own hair and then Eliza's. She followed Martha to the shed to fetch the buckets.

As soon as they were out of the clearing, Martha said, "Do you think it's that fever the men at the mill were talking about?"

Caroline nodded. "Henry told me last night that it was bad in Watertown. That's why they came home early."

Martha bit her lip and began to walk faster. They passed the boys coming back from the river with their buckets full of water, and they all exchanged fearful glances. When the girls returned, they were surprised to see Joseph helping Eliza dish up the mush.

"Mother's in with Pa and Henry," Joseph explained without looking up. "We moved Henry down from the loft so she could look after them both at the same time. She told us to go on and eat without her."

Caroline glanced at the shut door to the

bedroom. She could hardly make herself swallow the food, but Joseph said, "Finish everything in your bowls. Mother says we must all keep up our strength."

Mother did not come out of the room until the dishes had been put away. Her lips were set in a straight line, and her hands worried at her apron. She told Joseph to hitch up the wagon and take it back to Mr. Kellogg.

"Ask him if there is a doctor in these parts," she said, and Caroline's heart sank. If Mother was sending for a doctor, it meant that Mr. Holbrook was very sick.

All morning Caroline watched for Joseph to return. She fed the four geese and the hens and brought the eggs into the pantry. With Mother tending to Henry and Mr. Holbrook, Martha took charge of the cabin. She told Thomas and Eliza to gather wood chips from the woodpile. She stood over the cookstove stirring a broth Mother had told her how to make out of yarrow leaves from the herb garden. When Mother finally came out of the other room, Martha offered to nurse for a while so she could rest, but Mother shook her head.

"It's best that you stay out here until the doctor comes," she said.

Finally, Joseph returned near dinnertime. He was out of breath from running through the woods. There was a doctor who lived on the far side of Concord, but he was off seeing other patients.

"The doctor's wife told me the cholera is everywhere," Joseph said. Mother placed a hand on his arm and nodded at Eliza and Thomas, who looked scared. Joseph lowered his voice, but Caroline could still hear what he said. "The wife said she had no idea when to expect him. So I went back to Mr. Kellogg, and he rode off for Oconomowoc. Said there's sure to be a doctor there."

Mother nodded her head and for a moment looked uncertain as to what to do. Then she wiped her brow and gave Joseph a pat on the arm. "I'd like you to stay close to the cabin this afternoon in case I need you."

Joseph nodded, and Mother went to check on the broth. She dished it into two bowls and carried them back into the other room. Eliza rushed up to Joseph and put her arms around him.

"Are Pa and Henry going to be all right?" she asked.

Joseph took her hand and led her toward the door. "Of course they are," he said stoutly. "Now let's go out to the woodpile. I've got some chopping to do, and you and Thomas can help bring the logs."

Eliza wrinkled up her nose. "I don't think I like carrying logs."

"You take the small ones and I'll take the big ones," Thomas ordered.

"I'm older than you!" Eliza called back, following her brothers out of the house. "You can't tell me what to do. I'll take the big ones."

"But you're just a girl," Thomas announced, and when Caroline heard an "Ouch!" she knew Eliza had slapped him. Martha went to the door and spoke in a firm voice. "You must be good and quiet today so Pa and Henry can rest." Eliza and Thomas hushed right away and went silently to the woodpile.

For the rest of the day Caroline and Martha tended the fire and made sure there was enough cool water in the buckets while Mother went back and forth between the big room and the bedroom. Sometimes Caroline heard Henry or Mr. Holbrook call out from behind the door, and their voices sounded strange and the words made no sense. Every few minutes Caroline walked out into the yard and listened for the sound of a horse coming through the woods, but all the long day there was no Mr. Kellogg and no doctor.

That night Mother had Joseph pull one of the straw ticks down from the loft. The girls would sleep on the floor near the hearth. Mother would sleep in the room with Henry and Mr. Holbrook so that she could tend to them when she was needed.

"I can help," Martha said.

"Me too," Caroline added.

But again Mother shook her head. "Thank you, girls. You're being a big help now." She looked exhausted, but she gave them a warm smile.

As she knelt down to say her prayers, Caroline thought about Henry's donkey grin and Mr. Holbrook's quick nod. Tears came to her eyes, and she felt a sadness wash over her. She could never forget the pain she had felt those many years ago when Uncle Elisha had brought the news that Father was not coming back, but the sharpness of the pain had gone away. Now the fear of losing her brother and her new pa almost made her cry out, but she bit her lip and wiped away her tears. She did not want to frighten Eliza and Thomas and make things more difficult for Mother. Quietly she climbed in beside Eliza and held her hand under the covers until they both drifted off to sleep.

When Caroline awoke again, the room was filled with soft morning light, but there was no sound or movement in the little cabin. Caroline noticed that the embers of the fire had gone out, and suddenly she felt that something was terribly wrong. She pulled back the covers and walked on tiptoe across the hardwood floor, pausing for a moment to listen. There was no sound. Slowly she opened the door to the little room. The quilt wall had been taken down. The covers on Mother's bed had been thrown off. Henry was lying twisted in the sheets, breathing heavily, but Mr. Holbrook was entirely off the bed, slumped on the floor. Caroline wanted to let out a scream, but she clenched her lips tight and her eyes shifted to the other bed. In the dim light she saw Mother lying on her back, staring at the ceiling with wide eyes, her own breathing heavy in her chest. She seemed to sense that someone was in the room, and she reached out her arm. Caroline rushed to her and threw herself on the bed.

"Mother!" she cried.

Mother's blank eyes searched the room, and when she tried to speak, Caroline saw that her lips and the inside of her mouth were a strange dark color. Her hands gripped Caroline's wrist as she worked to get the words out. "Water. Please. Thirsty."

Cholera

Suddenly Martha was there beside Caroline.

"Help me sit Mother up so we can give her some water," Martha ordered, and Caroline raised Mother's head a little while Martha held a tin cup to her lips.

Joseph rushed in to the other side of the room and lifted Mr. Holbrook onto the bed. Then he straightened Henry. He pulled the quilts back over their shivering bodies.

When Mother seemed more comfortable, and Henry and Mr. Holbrook were tucked back in, they left the room, closing the door so Thomas and Eliza wouldn't get frightened by seeing Mother sick. Martha told Caroline to heat the leftover broth on the cookstove. Joseph took Eliza and Thomas with him to get more buckets of water from the river.

"Why doesn't Mr. Kellogg come with the doctor?" Eliza asked in a whiny voice when she returned.

"I'm sure he'll be here soon," Martha said, but she looked at Joseph and Caroline fearfully. They all knew that Mr. Kellogg would be doing everything he could. If there was no doctor knocking at their door, it surely meant that there was none to be found. Still, there was nothing to do but wait.

Toward the afternoon, the sickness made Mother and Henry and Mr. Holbrook toss and turn violently in their beds, so Martha and Caroline and Joseph all had to tend to them while Eliza and Thomas stayed in the big room. Caroline sat beside Henry, trying to wash his face and arms with cool wet rags. His skin was damp and leathery to the touch, and Caroline couldn't help but think it felt more like Baby's wet hide than the skin of a boy. Henry thrashed about, hollering and whimpering. Caroline spoke to him soothingly, but Henry did not seem to know she was there. Beside him Mr. Holbrook shivered and shook even in the heavy afternoon heat. Several times Mother tried to get out of bed but fell back, too weak to move. All three called constantly for water, and yet when a cup was held to their lips, they could barely get the liquid down for all the shaking.

"Everything will be fine," Martha kept repeating, but Caroline became more and more frightened as the sun set and night fell once more. Outside, the hoot owl's *whoo-whoo* seemed ominous. Thunder rippled far away in the distance. Caroline sat beside Henry until her eyes began to droop and she fell forward, jolting herself awake.

"Go to sleep now, Caroline," Martha said, in a voice so like Mother's, it brought tears to Caroline's eyes. "They are a little calmer now." Caroline protested, but Martha said soothingly,

"We'll take turns watching them. I'll wake you in a few hours."

In a daze Caroline went to the big room. Dishes and cups lay on the table unwashed from the quick supper Caroline and Martha had made. Caroline could not remember a time when they had gone to bed without cleaning the dishes and putting them away, but now she was too tired to do the clearing up herself. She was even too tired to put on her nightgown, and so she simply fell into bed beside Eliza. She slept fitfully, and sometime in the night she began to feel a terrible coldness deep down in her bones. She pulled at the quilt, but she could not seem to get warm enough. A voice spoke in her ear. She knew it must be Martha telling her it was her turn to do the nursing, and she tried to sit up, but there was such a fluttering in her chest and such a pain in her head that she fell back down. Her eyes flew open, and she saw a blurry whiteness above her. She thought it must be a bird trapped inside the cabin, hovering over her face with a white body and wings. She kept staring at the bird until finally it disappeared.

Then she felt her body shivering in the cold, and as she shook, the pain grew worse. Her arms and legs ached, and her insides ached as well. There was a rustling beside her, and she heard voices again but could not understand what they were saying. Her mouth felt dry and swollen all at once. She suddenly wanted water more than she had ever wanted anything in her life.

"Water," she cried, her voice sounding strange in her ears. "Water," she croaked again, and felt a movement beside her. She was being lifted up. The tin cup was cold against her mouth. She couldn't seem to get enough of the precious drops of water. The fluttery feeling inside her chest grew suddenly worse, and she fought to lie back down even though she was still thirsty. She felt a coolness on her forehead, and it eased the pain a little.

After a while there was more light in the room, and Caroline knew it must be daytime, but she seemed to be constantly dreaming. Many times she saw the white bird hovering in the air, its great wings flapping. Then far in the corner of the room she saw eyes that seemed to change into the hoot owl's round, yellow globes. The yellow melted into red, and it was Reverend Speakes' fiery eyes peering at her through the deepest black. His voice rang in her ears, words about dancing and gold and sin and sickness. She tried to get away from the voice and the eyes. They seemed to make her skin burn hot. She pushed away the wool blankets that lay upon her, and then she was shivering again, the teeth chattering in her head. The pain seemed to be everywhere at once, and she began to whimper even though she knew she was a big girl now and shouldn't cry.

Again she felt a coolness on her skin, and she tried to smile, but even smiling hurt. And always there was a terrible thirst. Each time the tin was put against her lips, she did not think she would ever get enough water.

And then very slowly words began to make sense to her. She still did not open her eyes because of the pain in her head, but she could hear a woman's voice saying, "You must rest now, Joseph. I'll take care of everyone."

Cool hands were placed against her cheek and forehead and she was being pulled up again out of the dark. She opened her mouth, but what she was given was not water. It tasted bitter and Caroline tried to pull away, but the voice said soothingly, "There now, Caroline, drink it up. It's a tonic to help you sleep." Caroline knew the voice, though she could not think whose it was. Everything was jumbled up inside her head. But she opened her mouth like a baby bird and felt the bitter liquid go burning down her throat.

And then she fell into a great darkness. There were no eyes and no voices, only velvety black. When she drifted up into the light again, there was still a great thirst, but the pain was not so bad. Someone was leaning over her, and this time Caroline's lids were not as heavy, so she opened them and looked into soft blue eyes and a warm smile. She reached out and touched the face to see if it was real.

"Grandma!" she whispered. Her voice was

still funny in her ears, but she knew she was awake and not dreaming anymore. Then she was being swept up into Grandma's arms, and she wanted to stay there forever, leaning into that warm, pleasant softness.

"My dear child," she heard Grandma say.

"Did the white bird with big wings bring you here?" Caroline asked, and she felt Grandma's head shaking back and forth.

"Not a bird, my dear, but near like an angel," she said, and then she laid Caroline gently against the pillow and brought the quilt up to her chin. "Now you must rest."

When Caroline woke again, light was streaming through the windows. She looked around and could see Grandma's dark-gray skirt swaying slightly as she stood at the stove, stirring something in a big pot. Martha was asleep beside her on the straw tick, and so was Eliza. Their hair was matted dark against their heads, and their skin was the palest of pale, but they were both breathing peacefully. Suddenly Caroline remembered Mother and Henry and Mr. Holbrook.

"Mother," she cried out, trying to sit up.

Grandma was beside her in an instant. "Do not worry, Caroline," she said. "Your mother will be fine."

"And Henry and Pa—Mr. Holbrook," Caroline added, in case Grandma didn't know who she meant.

"They are fine. But they are very weak, just like you. You must all stay in bed awhile longer." She tucked the covers up again and kissed Caroline gently on the forehead, then went back to the stove.

Caroline turned and saw that Martha and Eliza were both awake now, watching her with eyes that seemed very large in their thin faces. Caroline reached out, and their hands clasped together under the quilt.

Joseph came in from the yard and smiled down at them, and then Thomas rushed in and sat on the floor beside the bed. As Joseph stirred the fire, he told them that he and Thomas were the only ones who had not been taken sick.

"A miracle," Grandma said from across the room.

"The miracle is Mr. Kellogg going all the way to Milwaukee to fetch Grandma," Joseph responded. "I don't know how we would have managed much longer."

"You were doing a fine job, Joseph," Grandma said, but Caroline could see the dark circles under his eyes. Grandma added, "Just be thankful to the good Lord that the weather finally turned cool. That's what helped get the fever down."

At first none of them could get out of bed. They had been sick for two weeks, and they were thin and weak. But as the days passed and Grandma fed them good broth from a chicken she had stewed and small pieces of fish and rabbit Joseph caught, they began to stir about the cabin on wobbly legs—all except for Mr. Holbrook. Caroline heard Grandma and Joseph talking once. Mr. Holbrook had been the sickest of all. The fever had left him very weak in the legs.

Mother was the first to come out of the little room, leaning on Joseph's arm. She came to sit beside the girls and hugged them to her.

There were tears in her eyes, but she was smiling. She tried to help at the cookstove, but Grandma shooed her back to bed. Soon Henry was able to help a little with the chores, moving slowly but grinning and teasing like his old self. When the girls were well enough to change out of their nightgowns at last, their dresses hung loose on their bodies.

"We'll have new dresses soon anyway," Martha said, and Caroline remembered as if it were years ago that Mr. Holbrook had come back from the Watertown market with new bolts of cloth.

One night they were all able to sit down at the table together over Grandma's delicious rabbit stew. Thomas asked if he could sit beside Mr. Holbrook, and Mother could not say no. Thomas kept looking at him as if he would suddenly vanish, and it did look as if Mr. Holbrook might disappear. His once-broad shoulders seemed smaller under his brown linen shirt. The bones of his cheeks and jaw were like knives cutting through the skin. His face was still ghostly pale, and he had to speak slowly because he became winded easily.

Caroline felt a warm gladness spread through her as she looked at him sitting at the head of the table. She realized now that she could not imagine the cabin without her new pa.

Before they ate, they bowed their heads, and Mother said, "We must be thankful that we are all here together on this day." There were tears in her eyes again when she looked up, and Caroline realized she had never seen Mother cry as much as she had over the last few days. When Father had not come back those many years ago, Mother had hidden her tears from everyone.

As they ate, Joseph told them how Mr. Kellogg had searched high and low for a doctor, but they were all busy with other cholera patients up and down the river. He had then sent a messenger on horseback to Grandma in Milwaukee and had later gone himself to escort her to Concord.

"I do believe that kind man would have

nursed you with his own hands if he had not had his own wife and child to see to," Grandma spoke up.

"Were they sick too?" Caroline asked.

"Thank the good Lord, no," Grandma answered.

"What about Uncle Elisha? Wasn't there cholera in Milwaukee too?" Martha wanted to know.

"Everyone is fine there," Grandma answered. "The fever had already passed through."

"Will you be living with us now?" Thomas asked.

"I will stay until you are all well again," Grandma answered.

"I guess there's not much room around here for us all," Henry said, glancing at the straw tick in the corner. "But come spring, we'll be building a new frame house big enough for everybody. Isn't that right, Pa?" He turned to the end of the table, and Mr. Holbrook's sunken eyes looked pleased.

"The good Lord willing," Mr. Holbrook said slowly with a nod of his head.

Even though they were still weak, Caroline and Martha and Eliza were able to help wash the dishes and put them away. Mr. Holbrook settled into his chair by the fire. Thomas sat on a stool beside him, proudly demonstrating with his jackknife what a good whittler he was becoming. Grandma exclaimed over Eliza's sampler and praised Caroline and Martha on their nine-patch quilts. Then she sat at the table and told them the news from Milwaukee. Uncle Elisha was still busy at his newspaper, reporting on the cholera epidemic that had run through Wisconsin and on the gold rush that was making everyone crazy. Aunt Margaret had joined something called a temperance league and went to many meetings about how to get folks to stop drinking whiskey. The cousins were growing big and strong, and the oldest wanted to be a newspaperman like his father. As Caroline listened, she tried to picture Milwaukee with all its bustling streets and businesses and meetings to go to, but it was hard to imagine.

One morning Caroline was strong enough

to go outside and see to the hens. Joseph had already fed the geese. Caroline wrapped her shawl tight around her and stepped into the yard, her eyes blinking against the morning light. Wolf dashed up to her, nearly knocking her down. He licked at her hands and yipped and wagged his long bushy tail.

"Good boy." Caroline laughed, kneeling down and letting his warm tongue wash against her face. When she stood up again, Wolf followed her closely, not letting her out of his sight.

It seemed to Caroline that she had gone to sleep in summertime and awoken in fall. All the trees around the little cabin had changed into their bright autumn coats. As Caroline breathed in the crisp air, she seemed to be looking at the world with new eyes. Everything around the little house was beautiful to her. The pumpkins sitting plump and mostly orange in the garden, the green potato vines running along the ground, the corn stalks standing tall in neat rows, the bee skep she had helped to make, the little cabin with the smoke tumbling up out of the chimney.

At the henhouse Caroline called joyfully to the hens. Their white and brown and red and black feathers were a marvel to her. The sound of their clucking and squawking made her laugh out loud.

"I missed you," she called out. "Did you miss me?" And it did seem that the chickens had missed her, because they gathered around, pecking lightly at her boots as she threw them the grain Joseph had left for her.

After she had taken the eggs to the pantry, she walked out into the bright world again. She heard Baby's bell at the edge of the woods and followed the sound until she was running her hands over Baby's soft hide.

"You've grown bigger!" Caroline said, and Baby startled a little at her voice.

She meandered slowly through the woods, following the ringing of a single ax. The squirrels chattered in the trees. The blue jays and cardinals dove through the air and twittered in their nests. Wolf rushed into the brush after rabbits but immediately came back to Caroline's side. When she reached the end of the little path, Caroline gasped. It seemed ages since she had come to where the boys had been working. There was a huge swath of empty space with stumps sticking up here and there along the ground. Joseph was swinging his ax, but Henry was sitting on a stump, his hands leaning on his knees.

"I'm still weak as a newborn calf," Henry said when he caught sight of Caroline.

"Grandma says we must be patient and we'll get a little better every day," Caroline said, moving to sit near her brother on another stump. The short walk had made her feel wobbly as well.

"We'll need to get better fast if Joseph is right about an early frost," Henry said.

Caroline looked up at Joseph in surprise. "An early frost?"

Joseph let his ax rest against his leg and pushed the loose hair out of his eyes. His brown hair had grown longer, and he now wore it tied back with a leather string the way Mr. Holbrook did.

"I've been watching the signs and checking the new almanac Pa brought back from Watertown," Joseph said. "It looks like Jack Frost may come a-visiting sooner than we'd like."

"But then we must harvest the vegetables right away!" Caroline cried, remembering when frost had killed their garden two years before.

"We've got a little time yet," Joseph said, squinting at the sky.

"Have you told Mother and Pa?" Caroline asked.

"I don't want to worry them till I'm certain," Joseph answered. "Pa is still so weak."

Caroline thought of how Mr. Holbrook still stayed in bed during the day when the rest of them were now up and about. She'd heard him tell Mother about an aching in his legs that wouldn't go away. He had sounded angry with himself, but Mother had soothed him, saying he would be himself again soon if he rested good and proper.

"We'll all work together." Caroline spoke her thoughts aloud. "Even if Pa isn't strong enough, we can all work together and get the vegetables in before the cold comes."

Thomas dropped the pile of brush he had been carrying. "I'm a big boy now. Pa told me so," he said, thumping his chest. "I can do the work of two."

Caroline smiled to see her littlest brother so fierce and proud and strong. After a while Henry stood up and swung his ax once more. Caroline left the boys and headed back to the cabin. Inside, Mother sat at the table with her hands in a big bowl while Grandma bustled about the stove.

"There you are!" Grandma said with a smile. "We're just about to make a special treat to celebrate."

"Celebrate what?" Caroline asked.

"Why, that we beat the fever, of course," Martha said.

Caroline moved closer and saw that the bowl Mother was sorting through was filled with small reddish-green globes.

"Are those crabapples?" she exclaimed. "Where did you get them?"

"Joseph and Thomas came across the tree while they were clearing last week, but we've hardly had a moment to think about them till now," Grandma said.

Crabapples were much more tart and tangy than regular apples. Caroline felt her mouth puckering as she remembered how she and Henry used to pick the crabapples off the ground on their farm in Brookfield and bite into the hard, sour fruit.

"We're going to make apple turnovers!" Eliza cried, clapping her hands together.

"But there's no butter," Caroline said. It would be a whole year before Baby gave any milk.

"We'll make do with what we have," Grandma said, her blue eyes twinkling. She told Caroline to take the apples Mother had divided up and wash them thoroughly. The rest of the apples would be put in a sack and buried underground until deep in the winter. Then they would be sweeter.

Together Martha and Mother carefully peeled and cored the little apples. Then they sliced and chopped. Eliza sprinkled the brown sugar and the nutmeg Mr. Holbrook had brought from Watertown over the apples and set them aside.

Grandma set the mixing bowl on the table and measured out flour and salt, and lard from the salt pork. She had Caroline wash up and then mix everything together with her hands.

"We'll let the dough and the apples sit for a time while we prepare dinner," Grandma said. Early that morning she had taken another of the older hens and plucked it and set it in a pot to stew. She and Eliza brought down some of the onions and peppers that had been hanging in the loft above the boys' heads since the summer harvest. Martha and Mother sat at the table and did more chopping, and then Grandma stirred everything into the pot on the stove. The room began to fill with the hearty smell of her chicken stew. Grandma had already made the johnnycake. It sat warming golden brown in a pan on the stove.

When the stew was simmering nicely, Grandma wiped her hands on her apron, and the girls gathered round her at the table. She divided the dough into two balls, then rolled one ball out flat. From the flattened dough she cut out a small square. Using a fork so that the juice would stay in the bowl and not make the turnovers soggy, she placed some chopped apples in the center of the square. Then she folded the square into a triangle shape and sealed the edges by pressing on them with the fork.

She went back to the stove and heated lard in the big skillet. While the first turnover fried, Mother cut the dough again, and Martha and Caroline and Eliza took turns making more little triangle pockets. When the apples were all used up, Mother took the juice and poured it into the vinegar jug. The girls stood by the stove, watching as Grandma fried the apple turnovers until they were a golden brown. Grandma set them on a plate to let them cool. She told Caroline she could dust them very lightly with more brown sugar.

Now the house smelled like savory stew and sweet apples all at once. As she took the plates down from the dish dresser, Caroline's mouth watered and her stomach twisted to taste all the good food. The boys came in from their work, and Mother helped Mr. Holbrook out of bed. He nodded his head at the bountiful spread on the table and said to Grandma, "I don't know how we would manage without you, Mrs. Quiner." Still, he could eat only half of his stew and part of his johnnycake because his hearty appetite had not yet returned.

Then Grandma set the plate of apple turnovers on the table. There was one for each of them. Caroline nibbled the flaky edges and slowly bit into the warm center. With the brown sugar coating, the crabapples tasted almost like regular apples, sweet and delicious.

Everything was so nice, Caroline forgot all about Joseph's warning of an early frost. But later that night, when they were all sitting around the cozy fire, Joseph cleared his throat. He told Mr. Holbrook about the signs he'd been watching and about the predictions in the almanac. Mr. Holbrook listened thoughtfully, nodding his head as Joseph listed the things that made him think the weather would turn cold sooner than normal.

"You're fast becoming a mighty good farmer," Mr. Holbrook said, and Joseph ducked his head, pleased at the compliment. "Sounds like we still have a few days yet. We'll let the vegetables ripen a bit more, and then we'll begin our harvest at first light on Friday."

"But Frederick, you're still not well enough to work in the fields," Mother said in a gentle voice. "You cannot risk getting sick again."

"I'm afraid there's no telling that to old Jack Frost, Charlotte," Mr. Holbrook replied, shaking his head.

"I'll be here to help," Grandma said.

"Thank you, Mother Quiner," Mother replied in a hushed voice.

"I'm strong enough to work for two." Thomas loudly spoke up, and Mr. Holbrook nodded his head.

"I do believe you are," he said with a smile.

Caroline looked around the room. Except

for Thomas and Joseph, and Grandma, of course, they were all still tired and thin from the terrible sickness. She thought of the rows and rows of vegetables and all the bending and picking that would need to be done. It made her a little dizzy just thinking about it. But she vowed that she would try as hard as she could. Old Jack Frost would not get this crop that they had tended to all summer long.

A *Helping Hand*

Mr. Holbrook had said they would begin the harvest on Friday, but the very next morning, Martha shook Caroline awake in the still-gray dawn.

"Joseph says we must begin picking the vegetables today," she exclaimed. "The weather looks to be changing."

Caroline sat bolt upright in bed, shivering a little in the unusually cool morning air. Mother and Mr. Holbrook were already up and dressed. As quickly as her stiff arms and legs would move, she changed into her woollens and dress and apron. Grandma already had the plates and mugs set on the table and was ladling out the leftover stew and fried mush.

"Something to warm our bones," she said in her cheerful voice. But as Caroline looked around the room, she saw that the mood was solemn. They ate silently, and as soon as they were finished, the boys jumped up and headed for the door. Mr. Holbrook moved more slowly. Mother helped him put on his woollen coat and thick muffler and work gloves. He leaned on Mother's arm as he left the cabin.

Grandma said she would wash up and see to the geese and hens and Baby. "Hurry along now, girls."

Outside, the sun was shining but the air was already very cold. Little puffs of white came out of Caroline's mouth and nose when she breathed. There was no frost yet, but Caroline felt in her bones that Joseph was right. Another day would mean the loss of their precious crops.

Joseph and Henry had already brought all the baskets and buckets they could find and set them on the ground at the edge of the first field. Mr. Holbrook was working in the cornfield so he could stand and would not have to kneel on his weak knees. Mother was nearby. Joseph had chosen the row with the heavy, fat pumpkins, and Caroline was happy to see that they all were a nice orange color. She knelt down among the potato plants, her skirt sinking into the soft earth, and pulled. It seemed to take all her strength, but the large brown potatoes popped out of the ground one by one. She shook the dirt off and set each one in her basket. Sooner than she expected, her legs and back began to ache. Her teeth chattered in the cold.

Martha and Eliza were not doing much better. They did not complain, but Eliza's little face was soon gray and pinched under her bonnet, and Martha's hands shook a little as she pulled at the turnips.

Grandma came out of the house with a warm jug of tea and made them stop working. She poured the steaming liquid into tin cups, and Caroline gladly wrapped her hands around the warmth. The tea made her feel a little stronger. Still, it was hard to go back to working. She had to stop often and rest on one of the many stumps sticking up from the ground. So did Mr. Holbrook. Caroline watched Mother help him to sit. Mr. Holbrook's face was pale again, and he looked upset.

"You must not be so hard on yourself, Frederick," Mother said.

"It's these legs," he answered back, and his voice sounded angrier than Caroline had ever heard him. "They just don't want to hold me up."

Grandma came out to the garden after she had put the jug of tea away. She took a basket and began to dig up the sweet potatoes. Caroline and Martha exchanged a quick glance across the rows. It was strange to see Grandma working among them. In Brookfield she had never worked in the fields, because that was men's work.

At dinnertime they all walked slowly back into the little cabin and took turns washing their hands and warming themselves by the

224

fire. Grandma had left a pot of beans simmering on the cookstove. She had put extra chunks of salt pork in it. Caroline was so hungry, she wanted to gulp down her bowl of food, but she knew Mother would scold her. She made herself eat slowly and savored each bite.

When they went outside again, they stared wearily at the garden. Caroline knew they had all worked terribly hard, but they seemed to have little to show for it. There was still such a long way to go. Joseph and Mr. Holbrook were watching the sky as it swirled a darker, more ominous gray.

"Best get a move on," Mr. Holbrook said.

Caroline was just picking up her basket and heading down another row when she heard the jingle of a wagon. Everyone stopped and turned to look down the path. There was Mr. Kellogg driving his team of oxen. Four men were sitting in the back of the wagon. As they drove closer, Caroline recognized two of the workers Mother had fed last fall and winter.

Mr. Kellogg waved an arm in the air, then called, "Whoa!" bringing the oxen to a halt in front of the cabin. Grandma was the first to reach him. Mr. Kellogg jumped down and took her hand.

"Good to see you again, ma'am," he said warmly. Then he turned and smiled broadly at them all gathering around him. "I'm glad to see every one of you has recovered from the cholera." He reached out and gave Mr. Holbrook a firm handshake.

"We don't know how we'll ever repay you, sir," Mr. Holbrook said, "for all that you've done for us."

Mr. Kellogg shook his head. "No need for repayment, Holbrook. I was only too glad to be of some help in your time of need." He turned and nodded, and the men jumped down from the wagon, shaking hands with Mr. Holbrook and patting him on the back.

"Well, I just finished getting my harvest in for the winter," Mr. Kellogg said, "and it occurred to me, what with this storm a-brewing, that you folks might need a helping hand."

Mr. Holbrook opened his mouth to speak, but no words came out. Mother said, "Mr.

Kellogg, you've given us so much already. We couldn't possibly accept—"

Mr. Kellogg gently cut her off with a wave of his hand. "Nonsense. What are neighbors for if not to give each other a helping hand now and then?" he asked, turning to Mr. Holbrook. "You did as much when you and Henry gave up work on your own place to help build the mill."

Henry looked at his boots.

"Someday we'll find a way to repay you," Mr. Holbrook said solemnly.

"My repayment will be to see you all fit as fiddles once more," Mr. Kellogg said. "Concord needs good folks like you if we're to become a proper town." He turned to Caroline, his dark eyes dancing. "And a school needs all the good spellers it can get, don't you agree, Caroline?"

Caroline felt her face blushing and her lips pulling up in a smile. "Yes, sir!" she exclaimed.

"Well then. It's all settled." Mr. Kellogg glanced at the sky and clapped his hands together loudly. "I'd say by the look of those clouds we've not a moment to lose."

Mr. Holbrook hesitated a little longer but then gave a quick nod of his head. He turned and led the men to the fields, Mr. Kellogg following close behind. Caroline watched as they picked up the baskets and buckets and began to fan out along the rows.

Mother stood rooted to her spot, watching the men as well, her eyes pooling with water.

"You are truly blessed to have such good neighbors." Grandma spoke up.

Mother wiped the corners of her eyes with her apron. "Indeed we are. But it is all Mr. Kellogg's doing. I know those men. They work for Mr. Kellogg, and they would not be here unless he was paying them out of his own pocket."

Grandma's blue eyes went wide, but she said nothing more.

"Now then," Mother said, turning toward the cabin. "What do we have to feed all these men, Mother Quiner?"

For the rest of the afternoon the girls helped Mother and Grandma around the cookstove.

They did not have any game, because Joseph had not had a chance to hunt that day. But they had plenty of beans, and they had salt pork. Grandma cut great slabs of it from the barrel to fry up. There was still no butter, but they would spread the corn bread with the hot drippings from the salt pork, and that was almost as good.

Every once in a while Mother or one of the girls would have to rest by the fire.

"I'm glad we don't have to pick any more vegetables," Eliza whispered when she and Caroline sat together warming themselves.

"Me too," Caroline agreed.

In the middle of the afternoon Mother gave Caroline and Martha two jugs of hot tea to carry out to the workers.

"That hits the spot, little lady," Mr. Blue said, winking at Caroline when she handed him a steaming cup. She waited while he gulped down the tea, spluttering as he burned his lips and tongue. Caroline still thought the men were rough and unmannered, but she was grateful to them all the same. Large baskets of potatoes, squash, pumpkins, and corn already sat along the edges of the garden. The men were nearly finished and it wasn't even dark yet. Caroline tried to imagine how long it would have taken to pick everything without Mr. Kellogg's help. She knew they would have been out in the cold field well into the night.

Caroline caught sight of Henry at the far end of the field working near Mr. Waters. As she drew closer, she heard Mr. Waters' gruff voice singing in a low chant:

> *"When gold was found in forty-eight,*
> *   the people said 'twas gas,*
> *And some were fools enough to think*
> *   the lumps were made of brass,*
> *But they soon were satisfied and*
> *   started off to mine,*
> *They bought a ship came round the Horn*
> *   in the fall of forty-nine."*

"You mean folks can get to California by boat?" Caroline heard Henry ask in an awed voice.

"Yessirree," Mr. Waters answered. "Now me, I'm no seaman. I'd rather take my chances over land. But there's many think the water will be a smoother ride."

"Where would a body get a ship from here?" Henry asked.

"Most of the boats are starting out from Boston or New York and go around the bottom of South America—that's the Horn," the man answered. "But I reckon you could also go down the Mississippi and leave from New Orleans. There's sure to be boats pushing off from there."

"When are you heading out?" Henry asked.

"First thaw, I'm bound for California, so long as Kellogg is paying the way," the man answered. "No news from the first batch he sent out as yet, but I'm banking on a wealth of gold out there. No stopping me come spring."

Henry grew quiet, and Caroline watched his face as she handed him the mug of tea. It had been a long time since she'd heard her brother speak of gold. Her heart sank a little. He had been getting along really well with their new pa, but now she wondered if he was still thinking of trying to go off to the gold fields.

As the gray light began to fade from the sky, the wind whipped up and the air grew even colder. The girls watched from the window, and when the men reached the end of the last row, they gave a great roar. Then they spread out and began carrying the baskets and buckets into the shed and pantry and root cellar.

"There's not enough room!" Joseph said, banging the door open as he swooped into the cabin. "Pa wants to know if we can put the rest inside the cabin with us until we figure out what to do with it all."

Mother put her hand to her lips. They had never had such a good harvest before.

"Of course," she said, glancing quickly around the already cramped room.

"Where do you want this, ma'am?" Mr. Blue asked as he ducked into the doorway.

Mother rushed to shift chairs and chests out of the way, and the girls moved to help her. The baskets of vegetables went into every corner of the little bedroom and main room and loft.

"We must think of some way to thank Mr. Kellogg," Caroline heard Mother say to Grandma in a hushed voice. Grandma nodded.

Just as when Mother had fed the workers before, the men all sat down at the table, and the girls and women bustled about, serving them. Mr. Kellogg tried to get Mother and Grandma to sit, but they would not. They filled his bowl with beans and gave him an extra helping of fried salt pork. Mr. Kellogg thanked Mother and the girls, and he wiped his mouth neatly with the napkin. Caroline wondered what he thought of all the men slurping their food and scraping their plates and talking with their mouths full.

"You've a fine load of timber, Holbrook," Mr. Kellogg said. "I could see it as I drove up. You and the boys have done a mighty job clearing this land."

"We were moving steady till the fever came upon us," Mr. Holbrook replied. He told Mr. Kellogg about the plans for building the barn and house come spring.

"If you're counting on having any logs left over, you might consider hauling them to Watertown," Mr. Kellogg said.

Caroline saw Henry's face scrunch up. She knew he would not want to go back to Watertown anytime soon. But Mr. Kellogg didn't notice. He took a sip of coffee and continued, "They're building a railroad from Milwaukee to Watertown, and they need all the railroad ties they can get. I hear tell they're paying good money for as many logs as a man can unload."

Henry's face brightened, but his eyes were still worried. "Is there any fever in Watertown?" he asked.

Mr. Kellogg quickly shook his head. "It left with the hot weather."

"Well, I reckon we could spare a log or two," Mr. Holbrook said, rubbing his hand along his chin and looking thoughtful.

Talking of Watertown suddenly made Caroline think of something. There were still four fat geese in the yard. Caroline knew Mother was saving one for a special occasion, like Christmas dinner, but surely giving a goose to Mr. Kellogg would be one way to repay him for all his kindness. Quietly Caroline went to Mother standing by the stove and whispered in her ear.

"What a fine idea, Caroline!" she whispered back, her eyes bright.

When the men had eaten their fill, Mr. Kellogg stood up and thanked Mother and Grandma for the good hot meal.

"We'll take our leave now," he said, picking up his hat. "I know you all must be tired from your long day."

"We'd be a whole lot tireder if it weren't for you, sir," Henry said.

As Mr. Kellogg and the men went out into the cold dark, Mother took Mr. Holbrook and Joseph aside and spoke quickly to them. They both nodded their heads, and Joseph rushed out into the yard. Mr. Holbrook looked at Caroline kindly and said, "Good girl. I don't know why I didn't think of it myself."

Mr. Kellogg was just about to step up into the wagon when Joseph came from behind the cabin with a large sack slung over his shoulder.

"We'd be much obliged if you'd take this as a small token of our thanks," Mr. Holbrook said as Joseph held out the sack.

"What's this?" Mr. Kellogg asked, turning back from the wagon. The sack gave two loud honks in response, and Caroline let out a little giggle.

"It's one of the geese Caroline raised," Joseph replied.

At first Mr. Kellogg said he couldn't possibly accept such a gift, but Mother and Mr. Holbrook insisted. At last Mr. Kellogg gave in. He put the sack in the wagon bed and turned to Caroline. "I'm sure it's a fine goose, if you raised it," he said with a smile that made Caroline feel warm inside. "I thank you. I thank you all."

Then as quickly as they had appeared, Mr. Kellogg and his men were gone, back down the wagon trail. Grandma dished up bowls for the girls, and they sat eating their beans and corn bread while the boys made sure there was enough hay packed around the vegetables in the shed and that Baby had enough to keep her warm in the cold night. Henry loaded the wood box for the morning fire.

Each time the door opened, the cold wind blew into the cabin, cutting through Caroline's dress and shawl. At last everyone was in for the night and the door was shut tightly. The fire burned brightly in the fireplace.

"Weather turned so fast, I didn't get a chance to chink up the cabin good and proper," Mr. Holbrook said as he sat in his chair with his pipe.

It was true that the cabin was colder in the corners, but it still felt cozy in the middle near the fire. Caroline's whole body ached. She was too tired to do her sewing. They all sat quietly, listening to the fierce wind rattle the windowpanes.

"I know this house is much more crowded than you'd like, Charlotte." Mr. Holbrook spoke again. Every part of the little house was full of color, with all the pumpkins and beets and onions and turnips and potatoes piled in baskets. "Come next spring, when I have my strength back, the boys and I will build a fine house and a barn too, just like we planned."

"I don't mind a crowded home, Frederick," Mother replied, smiling warmly at him. "I'm just so thankful the harvest is in and everyone is well."

Caroline did not mind that it was crowded either. She thought of the long fall and winter ahead. There were no pigs and oxen, as they had dreamed about that summer. But just the same, there would be plenty to eat during the cold months. And maybe selling logs to the railroad would mean they would have animals roaming their land next year.

When Caroline woke in the morning, the air was frigid outside the covers. She stuck one hand out and then quickly put it under the quilt again. She snuggled closer to Eliza. She could see that the window was covered in a thick white frost.

Mother stuck her head around the door. "Come dress by the fire, girls."

Caroline grabbed her clothes and rushed to

stand beside the warm hearth with Martha and Eliza. Mr. Holbrook and the boys were already outside. Grandma had heated the water in the washbasin. The girls took turns washing, and then Grandma sat in the rocker and braided their hair just the way she used to do.

When it was her turn, Caroline smiled up at Grandma and said, "I don't mind doing the braid myself, but I missed you doing it."

Grandma's blue eyes twinkled down at her. "I missed it too," she replied. "There was no hair to braid at Elisha's house. I couldn't very well braid the boys' hair, now could I?"

Caroline giggled a little to think of Grandma braiding her big cousins' hair.

Soon the boys tromped in, their cheeks and noses red from the cold. Mr. Holbrook followed behind more slowly.

"Old Jack Frost sure paid a visit," Henry exclaimed. "It's a good thing we got everything in on time."

After breakfast they all put on their warm things and walked out into the bright white world to look at the garden. Everything was covered in a thick, furry blanket of hoarfrost. The grass crinkled underfoot. The leftover vines were frozen on the ground. The stalks of corn were bent down under the weight of the heavy frost.

"Mr. Kellogg came in the nick of time," Joseph said, and Caroline shivered to think of what would have happened if their neighbor hadn't come to help. Many of the vegetables would still be in the garden, rotting under the blanket of cold.

The next day the frost was gone, but it had left the grass and the vines in the garden brown and limp. In a few days' time, though, the sun had warmed up the ground enough for Joseph to dig a hole near the cabin. That was where they would store the potatoes they did not put in the root cellar.

First Joseph dug a pit in the ground five feet deep and lined it with hay; then he filled half of it with potatoes. He packed more hay on top and buried everything under two feet of earth. The potatoes must be kept cold, but not so cold that they would freeze. While Joseph dug, Mr. Holbrook whittled a long, hollow wooden tube that he stuck into the ground. That would make sure the invisible gas deep inside the earth would not build up and rot the potatoes.

Meanwhile Henry and Thomas took more hay and sawdust into the root cellar and packed it tight around the vegetables to keep them nice and snug during the cold winter months.

Mr. Holbrook and the boys chinked all the cracks in the cabin walls with mud. Then he showed the boys how to pack the hay all around the base of the little cabin with rocks so that the wind could not get in.

Grandma and Mother began to do the pickling and preserving. Caroline, Martha, and Eliza were busy all day long, chopping and mixing and minding the pots simmering on the cookstove. All the preserves and pickles were put into jars and crocks and sealed tight with fat. At night by the fire, the girls helped braid the onions into long ropes and the peppers into wreaths to hang in the rafters of the loft.

Soon the little house grew less crowded and colorful, but there was a wonderful feeling of its being packed full of stores for the winter. And there was the wonderful feeling of being well again. Caroline did not need to rest as often anymore, and neither did Mr. Holbrook. He still could not work a full day along with the boys, but his thin frame seemed to be filling out again, and every day he said his legs ached less.

In the evenings Mother cut and sewed the new dresses for the girls. Grandma told them more about Milwaukee, or she read to them from the book by Hans Christian Andersen that Caroline's other grandmother, in Boston, had sent them at Christmas last year. Sometimes Caroline and Martha and Eliza looked slowly through the *Godey's Lady's Book* they had nearly forgotten about because of the fever. The pages were full of beautiful ladies in velvety dresses and great satin hoopskirts, and little girls in tulle skirts and embroidered slippers. There were quaint poems and new songs to learn and announcements of important events back east.

One morning Caroline woke up and found the ground covered with a thick blanket of snow. As she went about her chores inside the cabin, she longed to run out into the fresh whiteness to play. So did her brothers and sisters. They were all restless as they sat doing their lessons after dinner.

"I guess you're well again, because you're back to fidgeting," Mother said, but her voice was not angry. She sounded pleased. She told them they could go out to play for a little while, but they must dress very warmly and come in as soon as they felt cold.

Caroline buttoned up her coat, tied her scarf around her neck, and put on her mittens, then dashed out into the wintry world after Henry. Her boots sank into the deep snow with each step. The air was crisp, but the sun was shining, making the clearing bright and glittery.

"Let's make a snowman!" Henry yelled, and

they broke into pairs to roll fat balls to make the head and body. Thomas helped Joseph make the first part of the snowman; then Eliza and Martha rolled another ball for the middle. Caroline and Henry made two smaller balls and together lifted them up and set them in place.

Thomas and Eliza went to find pieces of wood from the wood box to make the snowman's buttons, eyes, and mouth. Mother said they could have a bit of carrot for the nose, and they added sticks on each side for the arms.

Mr. Holbrook came outside for a little while to see it.

"A proper snowman needs a hat, I reckon," he said, and put his own hat on top of the bald, snowy head.

Henry put his mittens on the ends of the stick hands, and Joseph wrapped his scarf around the neck. They all stood back to admire their creation.

Then Eliza hopped up on one of the stumps sticking up from the snow in the yard.

"I want to make snow angels," she called.

Caroline and Martha and Thomas hurried to their own stumps. Even Joseph and Henry were not too old today to make angels. Caroline closed her eyes and fell backward into the cottony-soft snow. As she moved her arms and legs back and forth, she suddenly remembered her fever dreams about a white bird and fluttering wings. She carefully pushed herself up and turned to look at the six angel patterns spread out across the yard, glittering in the bright sunlight. Mother had said it was a miracle that they had all recovered from the fever, and Grandma had called Mr. Kellogg an angel for all that he had done to help them. But now Caroline wondered if there had been a real angel hovering over them inside the cabin, helping them to get well again, keeping them safe.

A Happy Christmas

The first snow did not last, but soon winter had settled in for good around the little cabin in the woods. All the trees save for the tall green firs stood with their arms bare. The squirrels were quiet and still inside their snug hiding places, and the rabbits had exchanged their brown fur for thick coats of white.

One day Mother announced that it was time to think about Christmas. She and Grandma began to bustle about the cookstove, making preparations for a wonderful feast.

A Happy Christmas

Caroline and her sisters were busy helping with the stewing and baking, but they were also busy making Christmas gifts. They were knitting new mittens and a new scarf for Mr. Holbrook, and they were secretly sewing handkerchiefs for Mother and Grandma.

One afternoon while Mother was in the root cellar and Grandma was resting in the bedroom, Eliza said she didn't understand why they had to make Christmas presents when Santeclaus was sure to find them again, just as he had last year, when he had brought the paper dolls and the buttons and the glass windowpanes.

"But Santeclaus doesn't give presents to grown-ups," Caroline reasoned. She had turned ten only a few weeks before, and she was feeling much older than Eliza. "Just think how happy Pa will be when he sees the scarf and mittens."

Eliza thought about that for a moment, and then a smile brightened her face.

As they worked in the cozy room, they talked about other Christmases. Slowly Caroline realized it did not hurt to talk about Father anymore, nor of the Christmases before he had gone away. It gave her a warm, contented feeling inside, like when she drank Mother's hot apple cider.

When Mother came in from outside, the girls asked her to tell them about Christmas when she was a little girl.

"Why, we did not keep Christmas at all when I was young," Mother said, putting the jars of preserves she had brought from the root cellar onto the table.

Caroline and her sisters stopped what they were doing and stared up at Mother in disbelief. There had been many Christmases when there had not been enough food for a big feast, but Caroline could not imagine a time when there was no Christmas at all.

Mother laughed to see their shocked faces. "In the old country nobody celebrated Christmas," she explained, "and so when your grandparents first came to America, they did not even think of celebrating Christmas."

A Happy Christmas

Caroline knew that by "the old country," Mother meant Scotland. Even though she had never met her Grandma and Grandpa Tucker, who lived far away in Boston, Caroline knew that they spoke with thick Scottish accents. Mother sometimes imitated the way they talked when she told stories about when she was a little girl, and it was hard to understand some of the words, though Caroline liked their lilting rhythm.

"But why didn't they have Christmas in the old country?" Eliza asked.

"Because it wasn't a tradition there," Mother replied.

"What's a tradition?" Eliza wanted to know.

Mother thought for a moment, then answered, "Something that is handed down from one time to the next."

"Like the little wooden boxes you gave us last Christmas that used to be yours?" Eliza asked.

"Exactly," Mother smiled.

"But if you didn't have Christmas, what did

you do all day?" Caroline wanted to know.

"Oh"—Mother shrugged—"it was just a day like any other."

Caroline did not like that idea at all. It was true there were always some chores to do on Christmas day, like feeding Baby and the chickens and filling the wood box, but mostly it was like Sunday, a day of rest. Only it was better, because there were new things to marvel at, like buttons and paper dolls and wooden boxes, and there was good food to eat.

"When your Grandma Tucker was a little girl in Scotland, the big holiday was called Hogmanay. It was the day before New Year's Day. Then there was feasting and gift giving," Mother continued.

The girls were quiet thinking about this.

"But Grandma and Grandpa Tucker celebrate Christmas now," Caroline said. "They sent us a trunkful of Christmas surprises two years ago."

"That is so." Mother nodded. "After they were settled in this country, they began to take on American traditions. But I was nearly

Caroline's age before I saw my first Christmas tree, and I was almost as old as Joseph before we began to keep Christmas at home."

Caroline knew about Christmas trees, even though they had never had one themselves. The Carpenters always cut a little fir tree and set it in their sitting room and strung popped corn around it. They also cut out little paper stars and moons and hung them from the boughs. The tree always looked very pretty.

"Can we put a Christmas tree in our house like the Carpenters?" Caroline asked suddenly.

Mother glanced around the little room. "I don't know where we'd put it," she said. Even with the vegetables stored away, the room was crowded, especially with Grandma there. The straw tick she slept upon at night lay rolled up one corner.

"Next year when we have our frame house, can we have a tree?" Eliza asked.

Mother nodded her head. "Next year then, the good Lord willing, we'll have a Christmas tree."

Caroline did not really mind about the tree.

There were so many other things to do. Last year she had made the special Christmas bread almost entirely by herself, with just a little help from Mother. This year Mother only looked on as Caroline mixed the dough and set it in the dough box to rise. The next morning Caroline took out the puffy ball of dough and kneaded it and let it rise again. Later she cut the dough into six long strips. She took three strips and carefully braided them together. She did the same with the other three strips. Then she made the special brown-sugar topping and sprinkled it over the tops. When she set the plump braids into the hot oven, she felt proud.

Mother set about making a plum pudding just like the Carpenters used to bring them. Caroline still missed the Carpenters very much, and so did Martha. They had received a letter from Mrs. Carpenter telling them news of Brookfield and saying that perhaps they would come for a visit before spring planting. There had also been a letter from Uncle Elisha announcing that all was well in Milwaukee and wishing them a happy Christmas.

At last it was the day before Christmas. There was a thick blanket of snow over everything. Mr. Holbrook and Joseph came in from the cold in the afternoon to warm their bones. They sat beside the fire, sipping the spiced cider Mother had made, and Mr. Holbrook helped Thomas chisel a small board of wood to improve his whittling skills. Later Henry tromped in, cheeks aglow, from seeing to his piglet.

Mr. Holbrook had bought the piglet on the trip to Watertown to sell logs to the railroad. Before the snow had settled in for good, Mr. Holbrook had again borrowed Mr. Kellogg's wagon, and he and Joseph and Henry had driven a large load of timber to where the railroad was being built. They had returned with even more stores and new shoes for Martha and Joseph, and Henry's little pig, which he called Hog just like all the other pigs they had ever had. Henry had also been full of stories of the railroad and how one day it would stretch clear across the western prairies.

"Imagine, Caroline! Someday it will take only a few days to get to California!" Henry said, and once more Caroline worried about how soon Henry would want to leave them for the gold.

For many days after going to Watertown, Mr. Holbrook had been very tired and had to rest often, but he was glad of the money they had made from selling their timber. He announced that when they built their new frame house in the spring, they would be able to have as many glass windows as they liked.

"As many as Mr. Kellogg has?" Eliza asked.

"Let's not get ahead of ourselves," Mother cautioned.

The night of Christmas Eve they hung their stockings and sat around the fire eating popped corn. Mother began to sing, and everyone—even Mr. Holbrook—joined in. Caroline thought he should sing more often, because his voice was deep and melodious as they sang:

A Happy Christmas

"The first Noel, the angel did say,
Was to certain poor shepherds in fields
as they lay;
In fields where they lay keeping their sheep,
On a cold winter's night that was so deep.
Noel, Noel, Noel, Noel,
Born is the King of Israel."

When it was time to go to bed, they all called good night and climbed under the warm covers. Caroline fell asleep immediately and dreamed of angels.

In the morning, Caroline woke to a roaring fire and the smell of Mother's hotcakes. She dressed as quickly as she could and rushed into the warm room with her sisters.

"Santeclaus was here! Santeclaus was here!" Thomas yelled, scampering down from the loft.

Caroline saw that the stockings were indeed bulging; and not only that, there was a brown paper package sitting below each stocking in front of the hearth.

"What do you think could be inside?" Eliza

whispered. "They're not square and flat like the glass panes last year."

But Mother said only, "You will know soon enough."

After the girls had washed up and braided their hair, Mother asked Caroline to go into the pantry and fetch the sugar syrup, now that there was plenty of it in a large crock. The syrup had come not from Mr. Kellogg's trees, but from the general store in Watertown.

Since Caroline had gotten the sugar syrup, she was the first to pour it over her hotcakes as soon as Mother had said the blessing. The fluffy hotcakes, stacked all on top of one another and drizzled with sweet syrup, tasted so good. There were also stewed blackberries from the summer and thick slabs of fried salt pork.

After all the delicious food was gone, the girls hurried to wash the dishes and put them away. Now it was time to open the presents. Mother told them to look in their stockings first.

Caroline reached her hand into hers and

found three patches of gingham to add to her quilt, a new shiny needle, and a thimble to match. Martha had the same, and Eliza had three patches as well so she could begin her own quilt. When the girls reached their hands in again, they each found a stick of red-and-white-striped candy and two more buttons to add to their collections. Caroline held her buttons in the palm of her hand and looked at them closely. One was shiny and round, made of blue glass that caught and sparkled in the firelight. The other was brown with black stripes across it. It looked like a tiny chocolate cake with frosting.

Joseph and Henry had new red suspenders and new blue mittens. Thomas had blue mittens and two more wooden men to add to his collection. Caroline brought out the mittens and scarf she and Martha and Eliza had made for Mr. Holbrook and wrapped in a pretty scrap of green calico. Mr. Holbrook's face lit up as he put them on. He declared that they were the warmest he had ever known.

"I helped make them, Pa," Eliza announced.

"Well, I'm mighty pleased. Thank you, girls," Mr. Holbrook said in his deep voice.

Then Martha brought out the handkerchiefs, and Mother and Grandma exclaimed over the tiny stitches.

Mr. Holbrook had made Mother a beautiful little writing desk out of carved oak. It had a perfect slanting lid that opened on metal hinges, covering a well in which writing materials could be kept. Along the sides Mr. Holbrook had carved a pretty pattern of leaves and vines. Mother ran her hands over the smooth surface and smiled. "Thank you, Frederick," she said, looking up at him with shining eyes.

Then she took out the gift she had made for him. It was a new vest sewn out of the dark-blue wool left over from the girls' new dresses, and it had a lining of cheery red-and-blue-striped cotton from Mother's sewing basket. Mr. Holbrook put it on over his brown linen shirt and looked very handsome. Caroline saw him clasp Mother's hands in his after she finished buttoning up the vest.

Then Mr. Holbrook cleared his throat and

gave Grandma the gift he had made for her. It was a set of carved wooden bowls, and Grandma thanked him kindly, looking very pleased.

Caroline loved all the gifts from her stocking, but she kept looking toward the brown packages wondering what could be inside. At last Mother said they could open them. Inside each package was a pair of ice skates! They were flat with shiny silver blades, and with leather straps and silver buckles to attach them to boots or shoes.

"Did Santeclaus know about the millpond?" Eliza asked.

"I reckon Santeclaus knows just about everything," Mr. Holbrook said.

"May we go skating today?" Henry asked.

"I don't see why not," Mr. Holbrook answered.

"After dinner," Mother said firmly.

For the rest of the morning, after the chores were done, the girls looked at their quilt patches and buttons and ran their hands over the shiny metal blades of their skates. Thomas

sat on the floor by the fire, making an army
out of his little men. Henry went off to feed
his piglet, and Joseph sat with Mr. Holbrook
talking about plans for next year.

When at last it was time for dinner, the girls
helped put all the steaming platters of food
on the table. There were mashed turnips and
mashed potatoes and rich brown gravy. There
was salt-risen bread and the Christmas bread.
And of course there was the plump, delicious
goose with bread-and-onion stuffing. As she
bit into the juicy meat, Caroline thought of
the Kelloggs and hoped they had saved their
own goose for Christmas dinner.

Everyone ate as many helpings as Grandma
dished out.

"It's good to see you with your appetite
back, Frederick," Mother said quietly, and Mr.
Holbrook gave his quick nod.

After all that food there was pumpkin pie
and plum pudding. Caroline ate until she was
full. She didn't think she could move an inch.
But as soon as the dishes were washed and
put away, they all put on their warm things

and set out through the wintry woods to Concord, carrying their skates. When they neared the millpond, they heard the sound of many voices talking and laughing and calling out. The pond was full of folk ice-skating!

"Let's hurry!" Thomas squealed, rushing toward the pond.

"You'll first need to put on your skates, young man." Mr. Holbrook chuckled.

They all sat on stumps sticking up along the bank and buckled their skates onto their boots. Mr. Holbrook knelt down in front of each of them, making sure the skates were tight enough. Santeclaus had not brought skates for the grown-ups, but Mr. Holbrook surprised them all by pulling out an old pair he had in his satchel. While Mother and Grandma walked by the pond and watched, Mr. Holbrook glided out onto the ice with the children.

Caroline tried to imitate Mr. Holbrook's smooth movements, but her legs were wobbly, and she kept slipping backward. Mr. Holbrook was always there to catch her. He took her hand in one of his and Eliza's in the other, and together they slowly whooshed around the whole pond, with Martha following behind. After a while Caroline began to feel less unsteady on her feet, and soon she was gliding along without any help.

The boys raced about the pond, laughing and shouting. They did not care if they fell. They just picked themselves up and whipped away faster and faster.

The girls skated together in a little line. Caroline was so busy concentrating on her skating, she did not notice the Kelloggs until they were right in front of her. Caroline skidded awkwardly to a stop.

"Did Santeclaus bring your skates as well?" Margaret asked, and Eliza nodded her head happily.

Caroline was surprised to see Mrs. Kellogg on the ice. She had an arm looped around her husband's, and she was smiling brightly. Her normally pale cheeks were a pretty pink in the cold. She wore a long cape made of deep-red velvet with white fur around the collar. Her red-velvet bonnet was fur trimmed as well, and she carried a little white fur muff.

Mr. Kellogg looked handsome as usual in a long brown coat and brown trousers. A tall black hat sat on his dark curls. "Happy Christmas," he called, and the girls sang "Happy Christmas" back.

"We certainly enjoyed the fine goose you gave us," Mr. Kellogg said to Caroline. "It was a wonderful treat for Christmas dinner."

Caroline smiled. "I am so glad you enjoyed it," she said, trying to sound like Mother would sound.

"When we're all finished skating, you must come join us for some Christmas cheer," Mrs. Kellogg said.

Caroline held her breath. She had seen the Kelloggs' house only from the outside. She could not imagine how fine it would be on the inside.

"We'll go ask Mother," Martha said, and glided off. Caroline rushed to follow, leaving Eliza to skate with Margaret.

"But we have nothing to bring them," Mother

stammered when Martha had conveyed the invitation. "And we are not properly dressed."

Caroline looked down at her skirt under her woollen cloak. It was true they were not wearing their Sunday clothes, but they were wearing the new everyday dresses Mother had made for them. Caroline's dress was made out of the dark-blue wool, and it was still crisp and clean.

"We can't very well refuse such a kind offer, Charlotte." Grandma spoke up.

Mother looked at Caroline's and Martha's eager faces. Caroline hoped as hard as she could that Mother would say yes.

"Very well then," Mother said finally.

Caroline's heart raced. She and Martha rushed back to tell the Kelloggs that they would be glad to join them. For the rest of the afternoon Caroline zigzagged back and forth across the pond. Eliza skated with Margaret, while Caroline and Martha became friendly with two sisters with long blond braids and round rosy cheeks. Their names were Hilda and Birgitta, and they came from Germany like Caroline's friend Elsa from Brookfield. But unlike Elsa's, their English was already very good. They spoke with only a trace of an accent, but they said "Ya" instead of "Yes." They lived on the other side of Concord, and they too hoped there would be a schoolhouse soon.

"Perhaps we'll see you in school in the spring," Hilda called as they skated off to join their parents, who were ready to leave.

Soon Mother was also calling to them from the bank. Mr. Holbrook and Mr. Kellogg had already taken off their skates and were standing beside the ladies. Mr. Kellogg led the way to his sleigh.

"There's enough room for the ladies to ride, but the fellows will have to walk," Mr. Kellogg announced.

"We get to ride in a sleigh!" Eliza whispered happily, and Caroline felt just as excited as she looked at the fine black sleigh with two brown horses waiting to whisk them away. As she stepped up over the runners, she could tell Henry was disappointed not to be riding as well.

The sleigh was cramped with all the skirts, but cozy. As soon as they were settled, Mr. Kellogg put buffalo robes on their knees to keep them warm. Then he picked up the reins, and the world was rushing by, faster than Caroline had gone on her skates. Trees and cabins flashed by, and the crisp air whipped and stung at Caroline's face, but she didn't mind. They left the main road and were soon climbing up and up, to the Kelloggs' grand house on the hill. It felt to Caroline as if she were flying.

Too soon they stopped in front of the large porch and tall gleaming windows.

"Come in, come in!" Mrs. Kellogg called as her husband helped her out of the sleigh. "The wind up here is merciless. I don't know what possessed my husband to build on such a hill. Sometimes I think the wind will blow me and Margaret away."

Mr. Kellogg went to see to the horses, while the ladies hurried into the house, wiping their boots and taking off their wraps. Even if she had had to, Caroline could not have said a word as they were led down a long hallway into the sitting room. She had been in such a grand house only once before, and that was over two years ago when Mrs. Stoddard had held the maple frolic in Brookfield. The Kelloggs' house was even larger than Mrs. Stoddard's.

Mrs. Kellogg opened two tall doors. "Here we are!" she said. Caroline almost gasped. The sitting room was as big as their whole little cabin. The walls were covered in a beautiful stenciled pattern of delicate tea roses, and there were velvety drapes hanging over the large windows. Two plush rose-colored sofas with shiny dark wood frames sat in the middle of the room. There was a mahogany table and chair set in one corner, a piano in the other. On the large mantel sat a mahogany clock and silver candlesticks. And above the mantel there hung a large portrait of Mrs. Kellogg looking regal in a dress of rich burgundy.

Caroline looked at everything and did not know what to do. She could not imagine sitting on such lovely furniture. But Mrs. Kellogg did tell them to sit, and so they did. Mother insisted that she help Mrs. Kellogg with the refreshments, and the girls were left with Grandma. Margaret took Eliza off to show her her room and her dolls. Caroline longed to go, but she knew she was older now. She must sit with Grandma and Martha and act like a lady.

Neither Martha nor Caroline said a word. They looked at all the fine things around them and then looked at each other. They could not imagine living in such a fine house.

At last Mr. Kellogg came in from seeing to the horses, and Mr. Holbrook and the boys were with him. Henry and Joseph sat down and looked hungry, while the two men began talking about plans for raising the school in the spring.

Caroline's ears perked up. "Where will the school be?" she asked when the men had stopped speaking.

"I suspect the best place will be in the clearing where Camp Meeting was held," Mr. Kellogg answered.

Caroline nodded. Camp Meeting seemed so long ago now. She wondered what Mr. Kellogg had thought of Reverend Speakes and his loud preaching, but she knew she could never ask.

"We'll need to find a teacher once we're finished," Mr. Kellogg was saying. He turned to Caroline and smiled. "Too bad you're not older. I'm sure you'd be a fine teacher."

Caroline had not thought about being a teacher before. She had liked helping Elsa learn to speak English. And she thought of Mrs. Morgan, her teacher in Brookfield, dressed in pretty clothes sitting at the front of the class, receiving apples from her favorite pupils.

"I think I would like to be a teacher," Caroline said.

"Not me." Henry spoke up. "I could not stand being cooped up in a schoolhouse all year round."

Mr. Kellogg laughed. "Still dreaming of California?" he asked, and Caroline held her breath. She saw a look pass between Henry and Mr. Holbrook. Then Henry shook his head.

"Not yet," he said. Caroline let out her breath. "There's too much to do around here. But one day I reckon I'll head out west."

Mr. Kellogg nodded. "I believe you will, young man."

Then Mrs. Kellogg was sweeping into the room in her bell skirt of rich velvet. She carried a large silver tray. Mr. Kellogg jumped up and took it from her, setting it on the table. Mother carried a smaller tray with china cups and saucers.

Mrs. Kellogg poured eggnog into the delicate cups and filled the plates with cookies and candy. The candy was made from maple syrup, just like Mother made sometimes. Caroline set the plate daintily on her lap the way Mother did. She sipped at the rich, creamy eggnog and nibbled at the delicious cookies.

As the adults chatted, the light began to fade outside the window. From her seat Caroline could see all of Concord below them lit up in the soft glow from the sunset. She knew Mr. Kellogg must feel proud every time he looked out the window at the growing town.

Caroline did not want to leave the lovely room, but soon Mr. Holbrook cleared his throat and announced that they must get back to see to Baby and Henry's pig. Mr. Kellogg said he would drive the ladies home in the sled, but Mother insisted that they walk.

"Happy Christmas!" they all called as they put on their wraps and headed out the door, and indeed Caroline could not remember when she had spent a happier Christmas. They were all well from the cholera, and there were plenty of stores to see them through the long winter. They had a school to look forward to, and they had wonderful neighbors like the Kelloggs.

Together the family began to walk down the snowy hill.

"Look, Caroline, you can see the whole world from up here," Henry said, pausing and catching Caroline's arm. "I'll wager you could even see California on a clear day."

Caroline turned away from the view to look at her brother. "I'm glad, because now you can come up here and look at it whenever you get the urge to run off."

Henry laughed. "Don't worry. I'm not running off. Not yet."

Caroline knew now that Henry would not leave in the spring, while there was so much to do around the growing farm. She also knew that someday he would leave, because it would not be long before he was a grown man and he would want to go off into the world. It was hard to imagine, but Caroline knew it was true. It gave her a pang.

As the others trailed down the slope, Caroline and Henry stood a while longer on top of Concord Hill, quietly looking far off at the miles and miles of sparkling hills and fields. Frosted with a thick layer of snow, the tiny cabins and barns, houses and trees sprang up from the hushed earth, glittering in the falling light. The world seemed very big, and Caroline was glad that there was one little corner in all the vastness that she could call home.

Come Home to
Little House

The MARTHA *Years*
By Melissa Wiley
Illustrated by Renée Graef

The CHARLOTTE *Years*
By Melissa Wiley
Illustrated by Dan Andreasen

The CAROLINE *Years*
By Maria D. Wilkes
Illustrated by Dan Andreasen

The LAURA *Years*
By Laura Ingalls Wilder
Illustrated by Garth Williams

The ROSE *Years*
By Roger Lea MacBride
Illustrated by Dan Andreasen
& David Gilleece

The Little House

MARTHA
(1782–1862)

———————— Lewis Tucker

Lewis (b. 1802)	**Lydia** (b. 1805)	**Thomas** (b. 1807)	**CHARLOTTE** (1809–1884)

Joseph (1834–1862)	**Henry** (1835–1882)	**Martha** (1837–1927)

Mary (1865–1928)	**LAURA** (1867–1957)

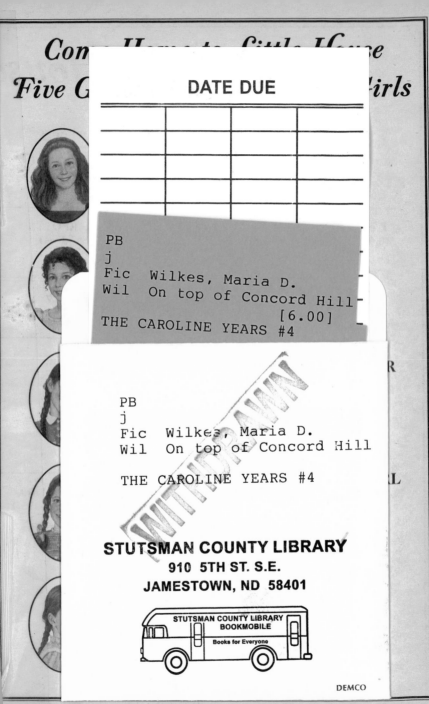

DATE DUE

PB
j
Fic   Wilkes, Maria D.
Wil   On top of Concord Hill
                    [6.00]
THE CAROLINE YEARS #4

PB
j
Fic   Wilkes, Maria D.
Wil   On top of Concord Hill

THE CAROLINE YEARS #4

WITHDRAWN

STUTSMAN COUNTY LIBRARY
910 5TH ST. S.E.
JAMESTOWN, ND 58401

STUTSMAN COUNTY LIBRARY
BOOKMOBILE
Books for Everyone

DEMCO